Unique Pen & Rose City Ink

Presents…

A THUG TAUGHT ME

How to Love 2

A Novel by,

Lady Lissa

&

Shelli Marie

Copyright © 2018 Lady Lissa & Shelli Marie

Published by Unique Pen Publications, LLC

All rights reserved. No part of this book may be reproduced in any form without written consent of the publisher, except brief quotes used in reviews.

This is a work of fiction. Any references or similarities to actual events, real people, living or dead, or to real locals are intended to give the novel a sense of reality. Any similarity in other names, characters, places, and incidents are entirely coincidental.

Recap from Book 1

Alondra

"Stay yo' ass right here and let me see what the fuck is going on!" De'vonte insisted, leaving me standing there with the principal slut. That bitch had the nerve to eye me up and down.

Soon as the door opened, the strong stench of weed invaded my nose. My nerves were wrecked with just the thought of what my son was doing in there, especially when his father started screaming.

Both me and Miss Parker went running inside the house. My mouth fell open when I entered the room and saw Javion dressed in only his boxers and some young chick in her panties. Titties just a bouncing and them muthafuckas were bigger than mine!

Glancing down at the floor, I saw two opened condoms. I immediately lost it. "You are thirteen fucking years old! Nigga, you tryna have babies?"

"I used a rubber ma', damn!"

Whack!

I must've slapped the taste out of Javion's mouth before De'vonte picked me up off my feet and took me out the room. I was fighting him the whole time.

"Chill the fuck out and let me handle this shit!" he snapped, pushing me forcefully into the living room. "Give me five minutes then we can all sit down and talk about it."

All that shit sounded real good until Miss Parker escorted the little girl out the room and sat her in the chair across from me. "Melinda, does your mother know you're over here?"

"Oh, you know this lil fast ass heffa?" I snapped not giving a fuck who she was.

"She's a good student who just made a bad decision!" Miss Parker snapped like she had an attitude... Miss Goody Two Shoes Bitch!

"Whatever she is, she wasn't being so good tonight! Her ass was in there half naked with my son! And with two used condoms on his floor, it doesn't take a fucking genius to figure out what the two of them were doing in there. They were fucking!" I yelled becoming upset all over again. "Lil girl, how old are you?"

"13," the young girl said through trembling lips.

"13, you're both only 13 years old what the hell do y'all know about sex! Please tell me what the fuck y'all know about having sex!"

She sat there quietly, as did the ho'ish principal. She had better keep her mouth shut with the way that I was feeling right now. I waited a couple of minutes for the girl to respond, but she didn't.

"I'll tell you what y'all know... not a damn thing! I bet you didn't know that even with a condom, you can still get pregnant. Did you know that?" I asked as I narrowed my eyes at her.

She shook her head no as she stared at her hands in her lap. She looked scared as hell but ask me did I give a fuck because I didn't. These kids were making grown folk decisions that neither one of them were prepared for.

Suddenly De'vonte and Javion appeared from the back room. I looked at my son and could tell he wanted to cry. I wondered if his father had finally whooped his ass because Lord knew he needed that shit.

"Yo ass is gonna stay right here until this lil girl's mama comes to get her!" De'vonte snapped harshly.

"I live with my grandma, but she's working right now…"

"Well, where is your mother, father, aunt, uncle, cousin, I don't really give a fuck who comes! You better call somebody to come claim yo lil underage fast ass!" I shouted getting up in her face.

That little bitch hurried up and snatched her cell out and dialed her mother. "Can you come get me?"

She had the nerve to be whining like a big ass baby right after being grown and fucking! These kids these days didn't have an ounce of common sense.

"She's coming. She said she's right down the street."

"Are you sure it's okay to go with your mother? I know your grandmother has custody of you…"

"Temporary custody of me. My mom doesn't beat me or anything like that. I just don't like her boyfriend that lives with her."

As Melinda went on and on, feeding us with the bullshit, there was a knock at the door. Since they were so wrapped up in the little girl's sob story, I went to answer the door myself. I knew it wasn't nobody but the child's mother coming to pick her grown ass up.

Thinking I was about to let the woman have it when I swung the door open, I got the surprise of my life. "Bitch, what the fuck are you doing here?"

Huffing and puffing, I began yelling at the top of my lungs ready to fight this bitch on my baby daddy's doorstep. The ho' was so lucky De'vonte came up behind me and took control of the situation. If he hadn't stopped me, so help me God, that bitch would've gotten the business.

"What the fuck she doing here?" De'vonte asked me. How the fuck would I know what that bitch was doing at his place.

"I came to get my daughter, Melinda…"

Everyone in the room became silent. Just when I thought things couldn't get more complicated…

Chapter One

Alondra

Nothing prepared me for what was on the other side of that door. When I opened it, I was dazed and confused to the tenth power. I mean, what the hell was this bitch doing on the doorstep of my baby daddy's place? As I stared into her face, I demanded to know why the hell she was here. I said a quick and silent prayer that she wouldn't say she was screwing De'vonte because if that was the case, somebody would have to call the laws on this one. When she said she had come by to pick up her daughter, I almost hit the fucking floor. I turned to look at the skinny little hoochie sitting on the sofa, I could definitely see a resemblance.

My mouth was sitting directly on the floor. I wanted to punch the shit out of Sadie, but I knew that wouldn't solve shit. I had to let her in, so I could let her know how her fast ass lil bitch was fucking my kid.

"You gon' let me in or what?" she asked with a sneer.

"I want nothing more than to kick you in the face and send you on your way…" I hissed.

"Then do it bitch! If you ain't gonna kick me in the face, step aside so I can get my child and take her home!" she said.

That right there made me wanna haul off and smack her ass. "Let the chick in!" De'vonte bellowed from behind me.

I had no choice but to step aside. After all, this was his house. I let that Sadie bitch walk past me, keeping my cool. Lord knew all I wanted was to grab her by her ol' crusty head and slam it against the wall. She waddled into the living room and I followed behind her. I needed to let her know that I wouldn't put up with her lil heffa fucking my child, all the while hoping that lil bitch was on the pill.

"Melinda Renee Brown, what the hell are you doing here without permission or adult supervision?" Sadie asked her daughter trying to sound educated with her hood ass.

"What do you care?" Melinda asked her mom.

"Little girl, I will wipe the flo' witcho ass!" Sadie retorted letting the ghetto pop right on out. That smart shit didn't last too long.

"Look, I don't know what kind of relationship you and your daughter have, but this is my house. Y'all may not respect each other at y'all's house, but y'all gon' show respect up in mine!" De'vonte said.

Umph, tell 'em zaddy! I thought. Shit, when he went into that aggressive mode, he always made my pussy wet.

"Melinda let's go!" Sadie barked.

"I'll go with you, but I'm not going to your house! I want you to drop me off at Maw Maw's house," Melinda demanded.

"You are not in any position to make demands on me. Now, let's go!" Sadie snapped bringing her lil brat to her feet. Her mama eyed her ass right back down on the sofa just as fast.

"I think we should discuss what happened here tonight between our children," De'vonte intervened.

"Discuss what? What, she's not allowed to spend time with your son?" Sadie asked.

"Spend time with my son? She was fucking my son!" I jumped in.

"Bitch get the fuck…" Sadie started to say.

"Ladies, I understand you're both upset…" Miss Parker interrupted.

"Wait… aren't you the assistant principal at my daughter's school?" Sadie asked. "What the fuck are you doing here?"

"Aye, aye, aye! Watch yo damn mouth in front of my son!" De'vonte ordered waving his hands around to give himself some room.

My pussy was screaming to get out of my panties, so he could rough her up. I loved when De'vonte spoke like that. I loved it when he used that tone. Shit, he didn't even have to be speaking to me for me to feel it down below. I wanted to grab him and shuffle him to the nearest room and fuck the shit out of him the way we used to. I hadn't had sex in almost six weeks, not even with Jordan. I was so done with his triflin' ass. All I wanted from him now was financial support for our kid. I knew he was gonna be pissed when I demanded money from him, but I didn't care. We made this baby together, so he was gonna have to deal with it.

"I was just asking why the principal from their school was here. I mean, if this is a family matter, she didn't need to be called!" Sadie shot back.

"Don't worry about why she's here! I just wanna know why yo daughter is here!" De'vonte shot back.

"Hell, I don't know why she's here! She was supposed to be at my mom's house," Sadie said as she glared at her daughter.

Her daughter seemed unbothered by her mom's attitude though. The glare that Sadie was shooting her were being shot right back at her ass by her child. I wished Javion would pull that shit with me. My hand was always itching to smack the heck out of his ass, so I wished he would give me a reason to strike him.

"Well, the fact of the matter is that your daughter was in my son's bedroom and they were having sex. What I need to know is do you have your daughter on birth control?" De'vonte asked.

"Dad, I told you that I used condoms!" Javion jumped in.

"Boy, if you don't sit yo lil' ass down!" I said as I hauled back like I was gonna hit him.

Of course, I wasn't going to hit my son; at least not with De'vonte standing right there. I wasn't worried about anybody else seeing me hit Javion. None of them would step to me concerning how I raised or disciplined my child… except his father.

"Alondra, calm yo ass down!" De'vonte demanded as he glared my way. Even though I loved his aggressiveness, I couldn't allow him to keep making a punk out of me in front of that bitch and his bitch.

"De'vonte please, Javion is my child too. The reason he's in this mess now is because you'd rather treat him as your friend instead of your damn kid!"

"What the fuck are you saying, Alondra?" he asked.

Aw shit! Now he was really mad at me. Oh well, it wasn't as if he was offering the dick these days anyway. He was too busy getting busy with his busty bitch. I didn't know what he saw in her fat ass anyway. I guessed he wanted an educated bitch because he definitely had the Section 8 and food stamp bitch already. I didn't give two fucks about being on Section 8. Hell, I had a nice house, well, not nearly as nice as De'vonte's but it was better than living in the projects like Sadie's hoodrat ass.

"I'm saying that if you disciplined our son more while he's with you, we wouldn't have to worry about him bringing randoms in here to screw!" I said as I twisted my neck.

"She's not a random," Javion said as he stared at Melanie all googly eyed and shit. "I like her… I like her a lot."

"Boy, shut the hell up!" I said. I didn't give a fuck if he liked that lil fast bony ass bitch. All I wanted was for these people to take their asses on home. I needed a conversation with Javion and his father, without an audience.

"I'm just saying that I care about her," Javion argued.

"You think she's gon' be arguing when I put my foot all up in yo lil ass? Shut the hell up, and y'all need to get the hell up outta here! I'm done with this conversation. From here on out, keep your lil fast ass girl away from my…"

"From your lil fast ass son? Gladly!" Sadie said as she walked over to the sofa and grabbed her daughter by the hand. She literally pulled the girl off the sofa and dragged her out of De'vonte's house. I wondered why she was pulling after that lil girl when she was pregnant, but shit, whatever.

I closed the door behind them and turned to Amerika's big ass; two down, one more to go. I needed to speak with my son and his dad and she wasn't part of the equation. She didn't have to go home, but she needed to get the hell up outta here.

Chapter Two

Amerika

"What did you just ask her?" De'vonte shouted towards Alondra.

"I told her to leave and let us talk!" his baby mama had the audacity to snap back with her hands on her hips. She was so damn lucky that she was pregnant because I was ready to temporarily forget that I worked at her son's school and whoop that ass.

Keeping my mouth shut, I watched the violent exchange of words until I noticed Javion turning up his face. He was on the verge of tears.

"Why do you always have to make a scene ma'?" Javion shouted getting in between his parents.

Now I was feeling totally out of place. I would've just gotten in my car and left but seeing that I rode with De'vonte over to his house, I was without a vehicle. What they were going through was totally a family affair and none of my business, but I wasn't about to have Alondra keep disrespecting me.

"You got this bitch over here…"

"No worries, I'm dialing an Uber right now! I can wait outside for it!" I snapped as I snatched my handbag and darted to the door while I pulled up the personal taxi app on my phone.

"No, you don't have to go anywhere Amerika! I'll take them in the den. You can go make yourself comfortable. You know your way around baby."

Out the corner of my eye, I saw Alondra turn pale as De'vonte's lips pressed against my cheek. Drawing away with a smile of satisfaction, I rolled my eyes and walked away.

As I passed Javion, I looked over at him only to see him nod his head and wink in approval. It was so cute, but his baby mama didn't think so. She let him have it soon as I left the room.

"Boy what the hell you grinnin' at Javion?!"

"What?"

They began going back and forth until I heard the door to his study close. Then I couldn't hear a word and I was glad because I knew Alondra had a mouthful of foul shit to say about me. It didn't matter much at the time though. Her baby daddy was feeling me.

With nothing to do with myself, I traveled to De'vonte's room and made myself a drink. I needed to relax after such a crazy night.

As I began to sip on the triple shot of Tequila I poured, I wandered into the closet and checked out De'vonte's wardrobe. "Hmmmm, he has pretty good taste."

Thumbing through the many suits in his formal section, I came across an unlocked metal box hanging off an upper rack. Being the nosy woman that I was, I carefully pulled it down with my free hand only to discover that it was much heavier than I thought it was and I dropped it.

"What the hell?" I gasped loudly as the large handgun tumbled out, causing me to spill my drink all over me.

Thinking quickly, I took a shirt off the hanger, picked up the weapon, placed it back into the box and returned it all to the same place. When I turned around and stepped out of the closet, I heard footsteps.

"Shit!" I hissed as I drizzled the drops of Tequila onto the carpet, I set the glass beside it and kneeled down.

Soon as my knee touched the floor, the door swung open. "Are you okay? I heard a noise."

"Yeah, my clumsy ass spilled my drink all over me trying not to spill it and still dropped it. I'm sorry. I'll clean it up."

"No, it's okay…"

"Just point me towards the cleaner, please."

De'vonte laughed and told me that there was some Lysol Disinfectant under the sink then stole a kiss before heading back out of the room. "I'm about to put her out and put Javion to bed then I'll be right back in here. Give me ten minutes."

"No, take your time. This is a serious matter and I totally understand." I said batting my eyes.

Getting quiet, De'vonte smiled and nodded his head. "Damn, that's why yo' ass is special."

"I am?"

"Yeah, and I'm gonna make sure I show you. Give me a minute baby."

De'vonte knew just the right words to get me wide open. Everything he said to me touched me. Whether he was stimulating my mind or my inner thighs, that man had me gone.

"Let me get this shit up!"

Rushing to the bathroom, I got the rag and cleaner and got my mess up in the closet and on the carpet in the room. As I hung the shirt back up I used to pick up the gun, I slid the section of clothing to the right exposing a small black dresser. On top sat something else that peaked my interest, a cell phone that was now lighting up. Glancing down at the screen, I saw a portion of the message.

"The job is done?" I chanted as I got tempted to open it up to find out. Before I could even muster up enough nerve, I heard the front door close.

Fixing the clothes back the way they were, I quickly left out the closet and went over to the mini bar in his master bedroom to pour another drink. De'vonte walked in as I placed the glass to my lips.

"Damn, that bitch is really stupid!" he huffed as we listened to Alondra honk her horn over and over while leaving his property. "Childish as fuck!"

"Well, you can't change her, but did you guys at least figure out what to do about Javion?" I asked as I positioned myself in the plush recliner next to his bed with my drink in hand.

"Yeah, I'm making a doctor's appointment for him. I can tell him about all the risks he takes when he chooses to have sex, but that shit don't help. He needs to hear that shit from a doctor!"

"I can talk to him for you if you want De'vonte. I have all the tools for it along with graphic pictures that will scare the shit out of him," I laughed but guaranteed it would work.

"Okay, can you just stay the night and talk to him in the morning?" De'vonte thought he was real slick.

"Then what type of message are we sending him by showing him it's okay to casually date and have females spend the night…"

"I'm grown…"

"You think that stops Javion from looking at it differently?" I enlightened keeping eye contact with De'vonte. "We should cut all that out until we establish something more… something more…"

A bitch was at a loss of words and I honestly didn't know what to say. Leave it to De'vonte though. He had a good comeback.

"Until we establish something more exclusive? Something more stable? If that's the case, we can tell him that we are dating exclusively in the morning. Now come on now baby."

De'vonte got on me so fast, I barely had a chance to set my glass down on the side table. Next thing I knew, I was butt naked in his bed with my legs spread and in the air.

"Shit, if this is your way of persuading me, I think you might… ah! Oh! Shit!"

Screaming to the top of my lungs, I clinched onto the back of De'vonte's head and guided it in a circle until I climaxed all on his tongue. Slurping up my sweet juices, he trailed kisses up to my mouth, until his hardness pressed against the opening of my wetness. The warm sensation forced my hips forward, making the tip of his dick tease my clit. Thrusting back and forth, I worked it until his member slid inside of me.

There I was, fucking raw when just preaching about safe sex. I guess I thought the rules didn't apply to me. At least I did, until I felt the load De'vonte shot up in me. That right there was a reality check.

"We have to stop doing it like this!"

Pushing him up off me, I got off the bed and stepped quickly to the master bathroom. De'vonte was right on my heels.

"Why, my shit is clean! Why the hell you trippin' ma?"

"I'm trippin' because I'm over here having sex with you like this and I don't know who the hell you're sleeping with besides me! Not only that, I'm not on any type of birth control! We haven't been in a relationship long enough to even discuss kids besides the son you already have! Think about it De'vonte!"

The thick silence in the room let me know that I gave him something serious to think about. It took him all of two minutes to come up with some drag about how much he cared about me. If he wasn't telling me he loved me, then I wasn't listening…

Cleaning myself up, then gathering my things, I looked to De'vonte for a sign that he was ready to take me home. If he wasn't, I was prepared to take an Uber.

Glad I'm an independent woman!

Chapter Three

De'vonte

I was already dealing with shit from Alondra and the situation with Javion. All I was looking for from Amerika was some comfort and a great stress reliever. It was all good until her ass started tripping about us fucking raw. She got all in her emotions and everything. Gave me no choice but to leave Javion there and take her home.

When we got there, she didn't invite me in and I didn't ask. I cared about her with all my heart, but I wasn't about to be begging nobody for their time.

Figuring that Amerika just needed some time to herself, I left there and shot her a text to let her know that I understood how she was feeling. I knew females needed to hear that shit sometimes.

After she responded back with a heart and a smiley face, I hit her back and invited her to an early breakfast. She accepted and that was good enough for me.

"Who the hell is that?" I whispered to myself as I arrived back to my house.

I could have sworn I saw somebody in my fucking bushes. Hopping out the car, I rushed over there only to see the back of a figure hop the brick wall to the neighbor's house.

First thing came to mind was Melinda. *I know Javion ain't that fucking crazy!*

Hurrying my ass inside, I found my son knocked out. He was snoring and slobbering so I knew he wasn't faking it.

After closing him in the room, I went to get a drink. Poured a double, took it to the head and filled my glass again before taking off to the kitchen. By the time I got near, I began feeling the effects of the alcohol. That shit had me a little dizzy.

Reaching in the darkness for the switch to bring me out of the darkness, I got a surprise sudden enough to make me jump. It was my silent security system that lit up my whole backyard lit up. Dashing to the door, I swung it open and drew down.

"Who the fuck is back here?" I yelled aiming my gun ready to fire that muthafucka.

As I checked the back, I heard my doorbell ring. I wondered who the hell could be at my door at that time of night. "Is this a fucking set up?"

My mind was all over the place. Thinking the worse, I shot upstairs, got my extra nine and cell then dialed my boy up. "What's good Block?"

"Nigga, hold on," I whispered as I went to the front door and looked out the side hole. I wasn't about to stick my face up to the main one and get my head blown off.

The rain was coming down in sheets outside and my windows and glass were a little foggy. I wiped the peek hole clean with the end of my shirt sleeve and looked a little closer. I saw right away that it was that chick with the pink hair, Sadie. She was crying.

For some reason I was hesitant on opening my door. I didn't know what she was about. For all I knew that bitch could have had Jordan there to do some foul shit. I didn't trust it.

"What's up?"

"Melinda ran away! Is she here?"

"No, she ain't in here."

Thinking about the noise in the backyard, I immediately wondered if it was Melinda. Opening the door, I ushered Sadie to the back with me just in case it was her daughter back there.

"Melinda!" I yelled out.

"You think she's back here?" Sadie asked beginning to look around.

After a few minutes of searching, we both decided she wasn't out there. Just to make sure, when we went inside, I doubled checked Javion's room. It was still the same. A whole bunch of snoring and no Melinda in sight. I even checked the closet and under the bed.

"She's not in there?" Sadie asked when I stepped out.

That was when I noticed that her shirt was soaking wet from the rain. Her dark brown erect nipples were showing right through. Made a nigga's dick hard naturally.

"Let me get some towels to dry off with," I offered jogging off to the main bathroom to retrieve a few. While I was in there, I tried to suppress my hormones.

Now I wasn't attracted to Sadie in the least bit, but her standing there in front of me with her titties showing like that had me. I had to go take a couple of shots before I went back in the kitchen to give her the towels.

"Thank you and I'm so sorry for just coming over here like this."

As Sadie sniffled and began to whine, all the power went off in the house. It was storming outside so the first thing I thought about was a power outage in the area. Hopping on my cell, I pulled up my electric company app and checked.

"Damn, what the fuck is wrong?" I slurred feeling like I could barely walk. Yeah, I was fucked up.

"Are you okay?" Sadie whispered coming up in my personal space. So close that her breasts were brushing up against my chest.

"Yeah, I'm cool."

Backing up, I took a seat on the stool to gather my thoughts. Sadie was right up on me. I wanted to push her ass off, but when she dropped down and whipped out my dick, I let her. Shit, I hadn't even cleaned Amerika's pussy juice off yet. Just the thought made me fuck the hell out of Sadie's face, busting right down her throat within seconds.

When she finished, she simply stood up and smiled before walking out the front. When the door shut behind her, my lights suddenly came back on.

"What the fuck?" I yelled out in confusion as I struggled to put my dick back in before running to the front.

Snatching the door open, I caught a glimpse of Melinda running to Sadie's car laughing. Yeah, both them little bitches set me up!

I wanted to wake Javion up and get Melinda's number, but then I thought about it. I didn't want to put my son in my business like that let alone admit that I had been played by his girl and her mama. Nah, I was going to have to take that one to the grave with me.

I just pray those skeletons don't come back and haunt a nigga...

Chapter Four

Sadie

"Lil' bitch why the fuck you take so long to turn the lights on? Didn't you hear me kick the door? Or was yo' fast ass too busy tryna watch?" I yelled at Melinda as we sped off De'vonte's property.

"Eww! Trust me when I say that the last thing I wanted to do was watch you disrespect yourself. It was dark, and I couldn't see anything!" she insisted but was steady laughing like the shit was funny. "Just remember that you said I can spend the night and that Javion can come over too!"

"I remember! But I ain't about to let that lil boy come over here and get between your legs again!" I snapped with the taste of De'vonte's cum still on my lips. I knew that his legs had to still be shaking after the bomb ass head I gave him. Shit, I even ate the booty like groceries! Had that nigga shooting in seconds!

Knowing my skills were on point, I pondered on De'vonte becoming my king to come rescue a bitch. I had to get out of the projects one way or another. He was just what I needed, and I was going to pull every trick to do it. Just like I did to Jordan…

I had no plans to suck De'vonte's dick when my daughter and I went over there. I actually wanted the two of us to have sex, but then it started raining and shit, so I couldn't leave my child out there that long. I was just trying to secure my spot on the throne. I was tired of Jordan's triflin' ass. I needed a real man and from what I could see, De'vonte was that man.

"Wow! You can do it, but I can't."

"Look, I'm grown so I can do whatever the hell I want to. You are a minor. That means you have rules to follow!" I reminded.

"Well, I can't wait until I'm grown so I can do what the hell I want to!" she said as she crossed her arms over her chest in a defiant manner while crossing the damn line with her mouth.

"I'm gonna go drop you back to your grandmother's house," I said.

"Why? I mean, we're right by your place," Melinda argued.

"So? I can't have you popping back over to that little boy's house like that. What the hell were you thinking, Melinda? I done told you already about giving your cookies to every lil boy in your damn class!"

"So much you know... he ain't even in my class!"

"It doesn't matter. Stop fuckin' all those lil boys! That's the reason I sent you to live with your grandmother in the first place. Are you trying to get pregnant at 13? Because I ain't trying to be nobody's granny!" I fussed.

I was tired of my child disrespecting me and herself. I sent her to stay with my mom after I caught her having sex in my apartment. I loved my kid and loved spending time with her. It was just that the shit she was doing was just too much for me to deal with. Hell, I had my own life to deal with and it was no walk in the park.

"You're a fine one to talk. I mean, weren't you just sucking Javion's dad's stuff? You knew that I was outside, but you still got down on your knees and sucked him off! What kind of message are you sending to me? Hell, I'm just doing what I was taught," she said.

"Watch yo' mouth, lil girl!" I said as I glared at her.

"Watch the damn road before you kill us both," she shot back.

I wanted to reach over and smack the shit out of her but decided to just drive her ass to my mom's. If I smacked her, it might feel so good I won't be able to stop myself, but I didn't want to get locked up. I wasn't the jailbird type.

"Don't even think about!" she said as she cut her eyes at me.

"Lil girl just shut the hell up!"

"We ain't gotta talk. Yo breath out here smelling funky as hell anyway," she said.

Ugh! That lil girl got on my damn nerves!

"Yeah, you won't have to worry about smelling the shit no more either because I'm dropping yo ass off! There ain't no way you're gonna stay with me and steady disrespecting me! I don't give a damn what you hear me say or see me do! I'm grown! You do as I say, not as I do!"

That girl had the nerve to complete my sentence in a sarcastic tone. I sat there and laughed at her all the way until I pulled up to my mothers. Then I got aggressive and drug her lil ass right out the car, all the way through my mama's door. She was right there waiting on her with a belt. She didn't even speak or acknowledge me. My mama just snatched Melinda out my grip and began tearing her ass up. I wanted to stay and watch, but then I was taking a chance on hearing the bullshit when she was done.

That was just what she got for talking mad shit…

Chapter five

Alondra

After catching my son in bed with some lil fast ass chick, I wanted nothing more than to take the belt to his ass. Finding out that bitch Sadie was her mom made it all the clearer to me about why the girl Melinda was in bed with my son. That bitch was just like her mom, fast and loose. It didn't matter to me that she said she lived with her grandmother. She was still a lil fast and loose bitch. If we didn't start keeping a closer eye on Javion, he was going to end up getting one of those bitches knocked up. Over my dead body would Melinda have a baby by my boy! There was no way I was sharing a grandchild with Sadie!

Feeling overly anxious about the whole situation, I called De'vonte as soon as I thought he had dropped Javion off to school on Monday. We needed to talk about some things if our son was going to continue living with him. If he couldn't watch our son more, I'd just move Javion back here with me. I had already gotten rid of Jordan so if my son needed to move back here with me, I was cool with that.

I picked my phone up and called De'vonte. I hoped that he'd pick up, so we could discuss our son and I prayed De'vonte would listen to me. I had real concerns and I wasn't trying to have them fall on deaf ears.

"What it do?" he answered.

"De'vonte, I need to talk to you about what happened with Javion the other night."

"What you wanna talk about?"

"We need to talk face to face. This is important, so we should have this conversation in person," I said.

"I don't know if I wanna see you in person. Shit, every time we get in each other's faces, you trying to fuck."

"I'm not trying to fuck you, boy! All I want is to talk about our son… PERIOD!" I said. I was trying to be the bigger person when it came to our son, and he was acting real childish. "So, we gonna meet or not?"

"I guess if you feel your concerns are valid."

"Don't you think we should meet up after you caught our son having sex? I mean, he's only 13 years old! I think there's a lot of room for concern," I argued.

I guess that, "boys will be boys" mentality was what had him feeling that way. Dumb ass!

"I'm on my way, but you better not try shit. I don't need to be nuttin' on that baby's big ass head no mo!"

I just hung up on his ass. The nerve of him to talk about my baby. He knocked on my door half an hour later, so I let him in.

"What you wanna talk about?" he asked as he headed for my kitchen. He opened the fridge and pulled out a bottle of Budweiser Ice.

"Aye, do I go in your house rummaging in your fridge?" I asked.

"Nah, you be too busy trying to rummage through my draws!" he said with a laugh.

"HA! HA!" I said in mock laughter. That shit wasn't funny at all. "We need to keep a closer eye on

Javion so that the shit that happened on Saturday doesn't happen again."

"He's a boy, Alondra! He just wanted to experiment with a lil pussy. Hell, he used condoms!"

See, that was the shit I was talking about. How could we expect our son to do the right thing if he was just gonna stand by and say at least he used condoms. "I don't care if he prayed about it! He's only 13 years old. The only thing he should be thinking about is books and sports. He shouldn't be thinking about no lil piece of pussy or nothing like that. He ain't ready to have a kid, so he shouldn't be fuckin' nobody!"

"Okay, so what do you want me to do about that? I can't watch our son 24/7."

"I'm not saying you have to watch him 24/7, but you sure weren't watching him when that girl snuck in, were you?" I asked. He rubbed his goatee as he looked away. "You were across town or wherever the hell you were! Our son needs more supervision and the bottom line is, if you can't watch him, I will."

"What do you mean by that?"

"I mean, if you can't keep a closer eye on Javion so that shit doesn't happen again, he can move back in here where I can watch his lil hot ass!" I said.

"Damn! It's like that, huh?" he asked.

"It's just like that. I won't be a grandmother before I make 35!"

"That shit would be kinda funny. You would have a baby and grandbaby that's about the same damn age!" he said and cracked up.

I stood there with my arms over my chest as I watched him laugh like a fool. All I could do was shake my head. He was so fucking sexy, and I was trying my best to keep my pussy from reaching out to him. I just needed him to get what I was saying so he could move on and my body could start behaving again.

"I'm not laughing, De'vonte. I'm dead serious!"

"Yea, I know. I'm sorry, and I will start to watch him better. Okay?"

"You better make sure that you do because if I find out about any other bitches being fucked under your roof, I'll move him back in with me."

"I'll watch him because Lord knows he won't wanna live back in here with yo ass!" he clowned.

"He wouldn't have a choice!" I said as I eyed him down.

"Aight. Well, if that's it, I got shit to do!"

"Just remember what I said."

"Don't be coming at me like that. I ain't yo kid!" he reminded as he walked towards the front door.

I followed behind him and he handed me the empty beer bottle before opening the door. I almost shitted on myself when I saw Jordan standing there. The two men stared each other down as De'vonte walked by him. Jordan didn't say anything until De'vonte busted out laughing.

"You got a problem, ma nigga?" Jordan asked De'vonte.

"Whenever you ready to square off, just say the word, ma nigga!"

"Jordan just get your ass in here!" I demanded pulling him in by his shirt sleeve before I slammed the door. I didn't even know what he was doing here, but I didn't want him and De'vonte duking it out in front of my damn house.

Chapter Six

Amerika

A couple of weeks after the drama at De'vonte's house, I sat in my office thinking about where things stood between me and De'vonte. I had been through some shit in my life, but never nothing as ratchet as the shit I had been dealing with lately. I wondered every single day if my relationship with De'vonte was worth everything I was dealing with. I cared about him a lot, a whole lot. I just wasn't used to dealing with a man with a baby mama like that. Alondra was a piece of work. To top it off, neither of them were keeping an eye on their teenage son, who was starting to have sex. At 13, Javion was definitely way too young to understand what sex was.

But from what I had seen, his mom and dad weren't very good role models. Alondra and De'vonte had been doing some careless shit, sleeping around, having unprotected sex, bringing strangers to their houses, and all in the front of their kid. It was no wonder the boy was having sex so soon. I wasn't trying to insert myself into their business, but I was there. I guess I should have stayed at my house when De'vonte said he was going over to his house and Alondra was over there.

I was the one who said I'd go with him. I guess I was thinking I might need to be around to help calm everybody down. I had some idea of how I'd react if I was a mother and I caught my teenager in bed with another kid. Since I was the outsider looking in, I just thought I'd be able to provide them with some insight. I knew Melinda and she was a good student. I also knew that Javion was a good student. I wasn't sure why the two of them fell in bed together, but the fact that they were able to do that meant they had a lack of supervision.

I thought that it might be time to speak with De'vonte about that. Children that were Javion's age needed more adult supervision and guidance. De'vonte had been devoting a lot of his spare time to me, which meant that he was taking that time from his son. We could start spending more time over there and less time at my place. If he wasn't up for that, I didn't think we would be able to keep going in this relationship.

It was a Friday, so once I made it home, showered and was on my second glass of wine, I dialed De'vonte up. It was as good of a time as any to bring up some of my concerns.

"Hey baby, what's good?" he answered cheerfully as if he were out of breath.

"Did I catch you at a bad time?"

"Nah, I was just finishing up at the gym. I'm coaching Javion's lil' basketball team up here at the Boys and Girls Club. Can you believe he talked me into this shit? A nigga ain't played ball since high school!"

"Oh, yes, I love it! When is his first game?" I asked excitedly. De'vonte was impressing me once again.

"It's tomorrow. I'll give you all the details later. Javion is going to a skill's camp over in Beaumont this weekend with the other coaches. I was gonna go with them, but all this shit was last minute. They're gonna have another one next month, so I already booked our room…"

"Our room, huh?" I giggled happily knowing that he included me in on a family event.

"That's if you wanna come," he sighed.

"I would love too and I can't wait to go to his game tomorrow. I didn't even know he played basketball."

"Yeah, I didn't either until he persuaded me to come out here. I seriously thought he was bullshittin' until I saw his big ass in action! That boy can damn near dunk the damn ball, Amerika!"

The excitement in his voice moved me. Hell, I was anxious to see for myself.

"Well, I guess I'll find out tomorrow what kind of skills he really has!" I was so giddy and excited, you would have thought that Javion was our son.

"Yeah, we can talk about all this after I get Javion situated. I gotta make sure my boy is straight, especially after that lil mishap at the house. Trust me when I say that I've had my foot in that lil' nigga's back ever since."

Now that's what the hell I was talking about and I didn't even have to say a word! That shit was sexy as hell and his take charge attitude was turning me on big time.

"I'm so glad to hear everything is going so well, De'vonte!"

"Thanks, but too bad I haven't had that much time to kick it with you. Don't worry though. I'm gonna make that shit up to you, starting tonight."

"I'm kinda tired," I admitted lazily, not wanting to get all dressed up.

"I figured after a full week you would be. That's why I'm bringing the party to you, baby. Just be awake and have a lil energy left for me when I get there. You won't have to do much, but I do need you to participate," he teased with that sexy ass voice of his. Damn, I was ready for him to come right now!

"Okay, I'm here."

Those were the only words I could push out. My concentration was on trying to keep my hand out of my panties. My clit was throbbing for some attention.

"Give me an hour, and I'll be at your door."

"I'll be waiting," I chanted as I watched the screen until De'vonte hung up.

Placing my cell on the off-white lacquered nightstand next to my bed, I snatched up the glass, downed the Stella Rosa Black and poured another. Lifting my phone back up, I pulled up Pandora and set the station to Jill Scott Radio. They always played the right type of music, for the right type of mood. The mood that I was in already… a lovemaking mood…

Throwing myself back onto my bed after finishing my drink, I rolled over on my fluffy floral comforter and squeezed my thighs together. Just the thought of De'vonte joining me had my insides on fire.

Not able to take it much more, I flew to the shower and take care of myself. I must've been in there longer than I thought because before I knew it, the water was getting cold and the doorbell was ringing.

There was no way that a whole hour could've gone by!

Without thinking, I draped the oversized towel around my half-wet naked body and darted to the door. The droppings from my hair and legs created a slickness on the wooden hallway floors forcing me to use my core muscles to prevent a fall. Clinching on the wall for dear life, I pulled it together and walked the rest of the way to the door to let De'vonte in.

"Are you okay?" he laughed with his arms full of bags.

"Yeah, I almost broke my damn neck tryna get to the door," I admitted shamelessly as I brushed the wet strands of hair out of my face.

"Damn, yeah, you be careful and go ahead and finish up what you were doing. I'm gonna be out here setting up all this grub I got for us. I hope you're hungry because a nigga over here starving."

That smile along with those dimples got me every time! De'vonte was so handsome, oh, and let me not forget sexy!

"Give me five minutes…"

"You look beautiful, so I don't see what you have to go do…"

"Thanks, De'vonte, but at least let me slip into some shorts and a tank top."

"Gotcha," he replied with a wink that sent that damn chill right up to my damn pussy! Why?

Rushing back into my bedroom, I dried off and threw my hair in a loose bun. Deciding to keep the mood going, I slid into a pair of spandex white short-shorts and my Michelle Obama tank with no bra. My perky breasts sat up perfectly in it and was just see-though enough to give him a little peek of my chocolate nipples.

Bouncing back down there anxiously, I caught De'vonte on the phone arguing with his baby mama. That fucked up my whole mental state...

That shit never fails!

Chapter Seven

De'vonte

When I got to Amerika's and saw her in just a towel with her hair all messy and wet like that, I wanted to fuck the shit out of her right there. The only reason I didn't was because my mind was somewhere else tonight.

Tonight, I wanted to seriously talk to her about being in a committed relationship. I was tired of all the other bullshit with my baby mama and the other bitches, especially Sadie. I couldn't get rid of the ho' unless I paid somebody and that was about to be my next step if the bitch didn't get the hint. Fuck that lil weak ass head she gave me, then had the nerve to lick my asshole so freely. What kind of freaky shit was that? Nah, that nasty trick been doing that shit to other niggas too.

I wasn't nobody special. That's why I took my ass right to the clinic and got checked out. I may not have fucked Sadie, but my raw dick went in her mouth! For all I knew she could've had herpes simplex or some shit. I wasn't taking the chance and I definitely learned my lesson after my that doctor's appointment. He ran down everything a nigga could've caught just from getting some innocent head. I couldn't believe it. I guess you could say that was why I went running to Amerika. She was the only female that I was truly feeling and actually could see having a future with. Shit, Amerika cared about my son and in my book, that was a fucking plus!

What always fucked things up was another female. During the past two weeks, I had been getting rid of all the chicks that were calling me and begging for my attention and dick. The only two that wouldn't get the picture were Sadie and Alondra.

Sadie, she was something else, but I had something for her ass. I was gonna sic one of my homeboys on her. I knew just who to throw on her lil thirsty pregnant ass.

Now Alondra, although she was my son's mother, she was gonna have to get the picture sooner or later. The only way her stupid ass was gonna get it was me showing her.

"Damn, speaking of the devil," I whispered as I answered my ringing cell.

"We need to talk…"

"We always need to talk, but now is not a good time."

Alondra went to the left screaming, which set my temper off. Next thing I knew, Amerika was standing in the kitchen with her hands on her hips. She was wearing a serious frown.

"Javion is at camp and he's fine. I'm not gonna keep telling you that shit, Alondra. Don't keep calling me about shit that don't pertain to our son," I spoke calmly, but kept my tone stern enough for her to know that I wasn't up for her games. I couldn't understand why she kept hounding a nigga for dick when she was pregnant with Jordan's baby. Made me wonder if she was doing that dumb shit when she was carrying Javion. That thought alone made me flash.

"I'm your only child's mother!"

"Not for long," I said fucking her mental all the way up. I had to turn off my ringer after that shot.

Looking up as I slid my cell into my front pocket, my eyes met with Amerika's. Those mesmerizing muthafuckas made me forget what I was about to say.

"Is everything okay?" she asked with a slight smirk.

Right then, I could tell that all the shit with Alondra was wearing her thin. I didn't blame her for getting fed up.

"Before we eat, let me talk to you right quick."

Grabbing Amerika's hand gently and guiding her into the living room, I gestured her onto the couch then joined her. Still clinching onto her palm, I stared into her eyes and began to explain about how I grew up and some of the shit I had been through. Reason being, I needed her to understand how hood love was.

"It's not the same as some ordinary love," I told her before kissing her lips.

"Well, who wants an ordinary love?" Amerika giggled playfully.

"You just have to understand, Alondra is ghetto as hell, but that's just the life we grew up in. It's just that I grew from that shit and she's still living in it. She's the mother of my son and for that, I love her, but that's as far as it goes. With you, it's different. I just wanna know if you're able to handle the drama that comes with Alondra."

"As long as you don't let her disrespect me…"

"Whoa! Now you know I would never let her do no shit like that, Amerika!" I replied with a raised brow. "We're in a relationship…"

"We are?" she gasped with a surprised expression.

"That's what I'm trying to get to."

"It is?"

"Yeah, I know it might be too soon to move in together, but I'm feeling you and I wanna see where this shit goes. I mean, you're an intelligent, beautiful woman that has the world going for her. Me, I'm just the opposite when it comes to our professions, but I've been doing some investing. Maybe with your help, I can get out of the game all together one day."

Tears began to stream down Amerika's face all of a sudden and I didn't know where the hell they were coming from. At first, I thought a nigga said something wrong.

"What the hell, Amerika?"

"I can't help it De'vonte! Shit, you are saying all the right things…"

"Well, shit! If saying the right things are bringing tears to your eyes, let's see what doing the right things will bring!" I laughed pulling her up to her feet.

Yeah, after this thug right here teaches her ass how to love, she gone be wide open! I'm gonna make sure of it!

That night, I took my time making love to Amerika. I had her body responding in ways even I had never seen! The connection was unlike any other shit I had experienced. I realized it when I got up the next morning and she was in my arms. That was the third time I did that shit!

The more time I spent with Amerika, the more I fell for her. Who wouldn't? Hell, her inner beauty was just as bright as her outer beauty. I didn't know another female that could touch her. Too bad Amerika wasn't that confident. I was going to do something about all that negative shit though.

"Good morning," she chanted rolling out the bed to rush and brush her teeth like always.

Going in there to join her, we went through our daily hygiene rituals together. It was something new for me, but it felt natural with Amerika.

After we finished, we went to the kitchen only to find all the food had spoiled and was now stinking up the fridge. We threw it all in the garbage can and emptied it before going out to eat.

Before heading to the restaurant, I swung by my place to change. Even though I showered at Amerika's, my shit was all wrinkled up.

On the way to my house, me and my girl chopped it up about our future a little. The conversation had me feeling hopeful about finally having a steady relationship. That would be a good thing for Javion to have some stability in his life.

That great feeling lasted all of ten minutes. Soon as I got there and saw Sadie standing outside, my smile disappeared, and anger now fueled my body. Amerika gripped my clinched fist and rubbed it gently.

"Don't trip baby, let's just get out and see what she wants. This time, please let me handle it." Amerika requested calmly peaking my interest.

Hopping out behind her, I tried to beat her to Sadie. "What are you doing here?"

"Oh, so you wanna act funny since you're dating the VICE principal of our kid's school?"

"This is my woman…"

"The bitch don't live with you, so that shit don't count!" Sadie shouted towards us with a fucked up attitude. I swear I wanted to punch her dead in her fucking jaw! She was damn lucky I didn't condone men hitting women!

"Oh, I don't?" Amerika laughed, dangling her own set of keys in the air to fuck with Sadie. Okay, I guess she did have a lil hood in her.

"What? You moved that uppity bitch in here with you?" Sadie asked as she rolled her eyes and neck. Me and Amerika both stood there laughing at her dumb ass before we left her standing there looking out of place.

"You wanna act like that?" Sadie hollered at the top of her lungs.

Knowing that she wasn't gonna do shit but try to tell on a nigga for letting her suck my dick, I drowned her out with a few loud 'goodbyes' before slamming the door. She wasn't about to fuck up the happy little home I was trying to create. Nah, that bitch Sadie didn't have shit coming.

Please don't let me have to pay somebody to take this lil bitch out! I know she's pregnant, but she gotta go!

As I walked to my bedroom in a rant, Amerika excused herself to use the main bathroom. That gave me time to call my homeboy up. I needed to put him on Sadie that same day. I couldn't deal with that shit no fuckin' mo'.

I'm gonna get rid of that nasty bitch, one way or another…

Chapter Eight

Sadie

"Oh, so now this nigga wanna square up and shit? He wanna choose that ol' stuffy ass bitch over a real hood bitch, huh?" I questioned myself all the way home only to find Jordan waiting for me when I got there. He was the last pain in the ass I wanted to see.

"What?" I snapped soon as I got in earshot.

"Don't be like that Sadie."

"Don't be like what? Am I supposed to be all happy and shit that you out there fuckin' different bitches every fuckin' night? Am I supposed to be happy about you bringing me diseases and shit?" I shot knowing that I could've been the one dishing it out to everyone. It was gone now, and I was clean, so I was ready to talk shit.

"All that's in the past Sadie," Jordan whined looking all good and shit. He wasn't worth shit, but that nigga sho' was fine!

"Well, it still hurts Jordan!"

"Let me make it up to you."

Pulling out more money than he did the last time, my eyes lit up. Getting thousands was much better than getting good dick. Well, for the moment it was.

"You just think you can buy a bitch, huh?" I asked sarcastically hoping that he wasn't going to change his mind about giving me the cash.

"I don't know. I thought you were already mine, but if a nigga gotta buy you, what's your price baby?" Jordan wooed coming close enough for me to inhale his sensual cologne. That shit smelled so damn good!

"Well, I gotta think about that one," I giggled and backed up.

"Take these five G's and consider it a down payment." He laughed before ripping my clothes off.

While he was doing so, I managed to stuff the dough in my purse that was hanging off the chair. I had to secure the bag before playing around with his ass. This time, I wasn't about to be the dummy...

****

Jordan whipped it on a bitch so good, he put me to sleep. When I woke up hours later, that nigga was gone and so was the money he gave me...

I hated when that nigga did some shit like that to me. No, that wasn't the first time he had dipped out on me with my funds. I should've known what he was up to since the last time, but I guess a bitch had to learn the hard way. Quickly wiping the sleep from my eyes, I grabbed my phone to call him.

"Wassup shorty?" he answered.

"What's up? Is that all you got to say?" I asked.

"What else you want me to say?"

"How about where the hell is my fuckin' money you stole from me?!"

"Stole from you? Girl, I ain't stole a damn thing from you in my life!" he said.

"That's a lie! You stole five racks from me earlier and I want it back!" I said angrily.

"I ain't steal that from yo ass. That was my shit!"

"So, why'd you give it to me if you was gon' just steal it back?"

What kind of game was Jordan playing? I was so sick of his triflin' ass, but for some reason I couldn't seem to shake him. He was like a bad habit that I just couldn't kick.

"I didn't give you any money to have, ma guh! I just let you hold it for a lil while, then when I left, I took my shit!" he clowned.

"Wooow! What kind of shit is that?"

"It's called ma shit! I got shit to do. I'ma holla atcha!" he shot before disconnecting the call.

"JORDAN! JORDAN!" I yelled into the already dead phone. "UGH!"

I screamed as I threw my phone on the sofa. I couldn't believe he had played me again. *Why did everyone in my fuckin' circle have to act the fool with themselves... Melanie, Jordan, De'vonte, even the damn pastor?*

Nothing ever went right in my life. How was it that everybody else was out there living the good life and I was stuck there in the projects, broke, down and disgusted. Jordan gave me five fuckin' racks but took them back when I fell asleep. How the hell could he do that shit and think he was going to get away with it? I had something for his ass though.

"I gotta to take a shower to wash the sex with Jordan off of me. I gotta get his scent off me. I need to find a way to kick that bad habit out of my life! I can't deal with his ass anymore. He's rude, disrespectful, and a fuckin' thief. Not only that, but my child don't like his ass." I huffed peeling myself sleepily from the bed.

Melanie and I hadn't always gotten along, but once Jordan became a permanent fixture in my life, things between my daughter and I went from bad to worse. It seemed like we argued for every little thing. She disliked Jordan and I got that. I just felt that she needed to get to know him better and give him a fair shot. I felt that she judged him too harshly from the jump. All she needed to do was give him a little time and eventually, things would fall into place. Unfortunately, shit didn't go as planned.

With my thoughts slowly disbursing, I unclothed and went to the bathroom. Turning on the water and waiting until it got to the right temperature, I eased in and positioned my pregnant body under the strong streams.

Suddenly, an eerie feeling came up on me. I couldn't really describe it, but I didn't feel right. Quickly bending down, I twisted the knob to 'off', and opened the shower curtain. "Shit!" I gasped deeply before I grew stiff. This dude was standing there with a gun dressed in all black. The first thing I did was open my mouth to scream. The dude rushed over and stuck the gun in my mouth so hard, he almost knocked out my teeth.

"Go head and scream," he dared through clenched teeth.

Well, how the fuck did he expect me to do that with the barrel of that gun sitting against my fuckin' tonsils? Tears rolled down my cheeks at the thought of this dude killing me. I didn't do nothing to nobody. I mean, I did, but nothing to deserve this.

"Now, I'm gon' take this gun out yo mouth and you gon' step out this tub. If you scream or try anything funny, I'ma put this bullet to the back of yo head so fast, it'll split yo weave in half. Ya feel me?" he questioned with a menacing stare.

I nodded my head, thinking that I could talk my way out of the situation. I was a smart chick and I had talked myself out of plenty of shit in the past. I was going to get out of this shit alive one way or another.

As the stranger removed the gun, I slowly stepped onto the plush bathroom mat. I was dripping wet, completely soaking the rug.

"Can I get a towel?" I asked as I shivered from the cool air.

Grabbing the towel from the counter, the intruder threw it at me. I felt kind of strange standing there, butt ass naked in front of a man with a gun who I didn't know from the man on the moon. Especially with his eyes glued to me as I tried to wrap the towel around me. Before I could secure it, the prowler snatched it out of my hands.

"You ain't gon' be needing that towel," he chanted stern enough to rise the hairs on the back of my neck.

"What are you gonna to do to me? Why the fuck are you in my place?" I challenged with a raised voice. I knew

I was taking a chance acting all bold and shit, but I had to get that man out of my spot. "Get out of my house!"

"Your house? I'd hardly call this piece of crap a house!" he said with a chuckle. "These the fuckin' projects!"

"Call it what you want, but to me it's a home! Why are you here? What do you want?"

"Well, I came here to kill your ass, but seeing that you wanna fuck…"

"The devil is a lie! I don't wanna fuck you! Shit, I don't even know you!" I said angrily. The nerve of that nigga, thinking I wanted to fuck him. He was okay looking and all, but I wasn't trying to fuck him. Hell, my pussy was already tore up from fuckin' with Jordan's dumb ass.

"Well, how 'bout you suck ma dick for now and we'll see about the fuckin' after," he instructed as he reached into his pants for his dick.

"Muthafucka, you gon' have to just kill me now because I ain't finna suck yo dick! I don't know where yo shit been!" I frowned and stood my ground. *He must be losing his fuckin' mind!*

"That'll work for me," he threatened removing his hand from his pants before cocking the hammer on his gun. As I stared down the barrel of his weapon, I realized that I wasn't ready to die.

"WAIT! WAIT! WAIT!" I cried as I held up my hands releasing my bare breasts that I was struggling to cover up.

"WHAT?!" he barked.

"I'm pregnant!"

"Duh bitch! I got eyes!"

"And you'd still kill me?"

"In a heartbeat! That ain't my fuckin' baby!" he twisted his lips pointing the gun back at me.

"Wait, I'll do it!" I had sucked plenty of dicks in my lifetime, which is why I was such a pro at it. I hurried up and prepared myself for the porno role of a lifetime.

"I thought you'd see it my way," he smirked reaching in his pants once again to draw out his dick.

I almost busted out laughing at the scraggly lil pencil dick he pulled out. *How could niggas be that fine and be working with such small dicks?*

I bet that was why he wanted me to suck it. He couldn't get much action with that lil pistol. I took it between my thumb and forefinger and closed my eyes. All I could think about was when the comedian Adele Givens with her full-sized lips compared her sucking a lil dick, to giving a whale a tick tack. That shit played over and over in my head as I took his little noodle in my mouth, and almost gagged to stop from clowning his ass. I swear it was like sucking a horrible tasting gummy worm.

After a few minutes, he pulled his member out of my mouth. "Bend over!" he said gruffly.

"For what?" I asked.

"So, I could fuck you, bitch! What you think?" he asked.

"I never agreed to have sex with you! I ain't fuckin'
that…" I stopped myself from saying what I really wanted
to say. I didn't want him to shoot my ass. Most niggas
didn't take it well when you told them about their small
dicks.

"Pregnant pussy be the best fuckin' pussy! Now,
turn the fuck around or eat this bullet, bitch!" he growled.
Hell, that nigga ain't had to tell me twice. I quickly turned
around and braced myself to fake my moans for fear of
getting shot.

I heard the wrapper from the condom being ripped
open and prayed that he had gotten his size. I'd hate for
him to try using a Magnum and lose that too big condom in
my kitty cat.

It took him several minutes to get his dick in and
keep it in. That shit kept popping out like a baby's pacifier.
It took everything in me not to bust out laughing. He finally
got his dick to act right and I started feeling a little
something. It wasn't anything that would make me call him
"zaddy" though. It was kind of like a tickle to my clitoris,
but I moaned a little, just light moaning though. Nothing
like I did when I got fucked by Jordan. I was hoping that if
I pretended to enjoy the sex, he'd spare my life.

After a few minutes, he hollered like a lil bitch and
his lil dick plopped out. "Damn! Pregnant pussy be the best
pussy!" Before I had a chance to say anything, I heard him
cock the hammer again.

"Wait!" I cried as I took off running with my naked
pregnant ass. I didn't know how far I was gonna get, but I
had to at least try to get away from him.

He cussed me out and fired a shot. The bullet whizzed by me and hit the wall in front of me. That nigga better quit playing like that. He bout to get me killed and shit. I was stunned for a minute but kept running.

POW!

Oh shit! That one hit me. The pain I felt in my arm was intense, but it didn't stop me from running. I was now in the hallway trying to make it to the door. The next pop I heard caused me to fall to the floor. I tried to get up and run again, but I could barely move due to the horrible pain in my back.

"BITCH! YOU MUST BE TRYNA GET ME KILLED!" he yelled.

"Please don't kill me!" I begged. "I'm pregnant and I have a daughter!" I prayed someone heard the gunshots and would call the police. Who was I kidding? I lived in the hood. People around here head gunshots every single day. That shit was the norm around the streets. Nobody in their right mind would care enough about the gunshots to call the cops. They'd just continue to go about their business no matter what they heard. I knew I should've moved away from there a long time ago, but that cheap rent was the reason I had stayed put.

"I don't give a fuck if you got a whole shoebox full of kids, yo! This shit ain't personal. I'm getting paid big money to take yo ass out, so that's exactly what I'm gonna do!" he said.

"Somebody paid you to kill me? Why? Who would do that shit?"

I couldn't understand why anyone would want me dead. I didn't deserve this shit. "Tell my grandma I said hi. She'll be the lady with the big mouth waiting to tell you all the business up there," he said as he pointed the gun at me.

"God please don't let me die," I prayed in my head before I felt the most intense pain I had ever felt in my life. A bitch didn't deserve to go out like that. I knew I had some work to do on myself with my attitude and lack of maternal skills and all, but damn... I wouldn't even be able to do that. Damn!

Chapter Nine

Jordan

I didn't know what the fuck Sadie was going off about. That ho' had a habit of thinking I was about to pay her for that ol' stank pussy. A nigga only fucked with her because she gave good head and shit, but I was tired giving her my fuckin' money. Plus, I was about to end things with her ass. That was why I was laid up there with my new girl, Jackie, at her place. I figured I'd give Sadie a few days to cool off before I went by there to get my shit. I was tired dealing with her ratchet ass. Jackie didn't live in the projects; she had her own crib and her shit always smelled good.

As my chick got settled in my arms, my hands began to roam over her body. She smiled as I kissed my way to her pussy. That girl was fine as hell, way finer than Alondra and Sadie's asses put together.

Now Jackie had some good pussy and it smelled way better than Sadie's fish stick kitty. I dove my face in that coochie with full force, licking and sucking her from the rooter to the tooter. I dove my tongue inside her pussy and her asshole. I couldn't help myself because she smelled so damn good.

Within minutes, Jackie was pushing me away from her pussy, but I wasn't done yet. I held her down and continued to lap up her juices like a thirsty dog on a hot summer's day a bit longer.

After I finally had feasted on her goodies enough, I slid the condom on my dick and prepared to enter her warm tunnel. I wasn't the type of nigga that liked to use condoms, but I had learned my lesson. I was tired of getting burned by these bitches out in these streets. My dick wasn't going to fall off because I was too careless. *No indeed.*

Keeping my focus as I slowly entered, I began to rotate my hips against Jackie's pelvis as she moaned in my ear. I loved when a bitch moaned and called out my name, but tonight I was in the mood to hear something else. Tonight, I was in the mood to hear her scream. I lifted one of her legs up on my shoulder and plowed deeper inside her kitty. I wanted to touch the bottom of that muthafucka.

Just as I knew she would, she started to scream louder. "Ooouuuu shit!" she cried.

"Take that dick, baby!" I demanded picking up the pace. I was now beating that pussy up as she hollered, and her body shook.

"Turn over!" I ordered as I pulled my dick out and allowed her to get on all fours. Wasting no time, I slammed into her ass from behind and watched the big muthafucka jiggle against my dick. *I'm gonna fuck the shit out of her tonight.*

Not literally fuck the shit out of her though because I didn't want no shit on my dick. That was one of the main reasons I never wanted to penetrate a bitch in her asshole.

The whole visual was throwing me off, so I dipped out her ass and back into her pussy. I stayed there until I nutted. By then, I was completely satisfied… at least for the moment.

Drawing the nasty condom of my stiff dick, I held it in the air for Jackie to dispose of it, right along with douching her pussy. I didn't want her to get a bacterial infection from me transferring that shitty condom to her coochie.

"Ugh," I sulked as I smeared my cum all over Jackie's panties she had left in the bed.

To get my mind off the shit, literally, I grabbed the blunt out the ashtray and lit it up. Taking a long hard pull, I exhaled as my cell rang.

It was an unknown caller, so I assumed it was one of my jump-offs. Since Jackie was in the shower, I went ahead and took the chance and answered it.

"Yeah," I started before becoming real quiet.

The call was from the police who were at Sadie's house. She had been raped, sodomized and shot. She was at the hospital clinging on for dear life. I couldn't believe the shit! I knew Alondra couldn't have done it because they said she was raped.

"We need you to come down for questioning…"

"You can question me at the fuckin' hospital because that's where I'm going! She's carrying my fucking baby!"

Jackie came flying out the bathroom, butt ass naked with her titties bouncing everywhere. "What's going on?"

"My baby mama got shot. I gotta go see what's going on."

"You want me to come with you?" she asked hurrying to get dressed.

"Nah, let me see what's up and I'll hit you from there."

Totally understanding like the good lil bitch she was, Jackie gave me a kiss and sent a nigga on his way. Yeah, she was a keeper.

Getting in my ride, my mind went straight to Sadie. I thought about how dirty I had just done her. Yeah, I was starting to feel a lil guilty and concerned about my seed. I just prayed that they were both okay.

I didn't wish this shit on her! Who the fuck would do something like that. Shit, who the fuck else was she messing with?

With my mind in a rage, I made it to the hospital in record timing. Only I didn't get to see Sadie or check on her. Reason being, I was greeted at the receptionist desk by Houston's finest.

They rushed to handcuff me the moment I spoke my name to the female clerk. They read me my rights and next thing I knew, I was being shoved into the back of a squad car.

The entire ride to the precinct, the officer in the passenger seat was dishing out threats while dropping helpful lugs. "You know the neighbors saw you there earlier today. Did you guys have a fight?"

"Nah, we ain't had no fight…"

"Well, according to Lucille Mason that lives right next door, you two were yelling and slamming doors."

Okay, so these muthafuckas gonna try to pin this shit on me? I got a twist for they ass.

I plotted silently as I listened to all the evidence they had on me. I wasn't a snitch, but I was about to shift their suspicion to someone else. Someone I was waiting to pay back.

"So, you don't know who else could've done something so inhumane?" the female cop asked once I got to the station and shoved into an interrogation room.

"Look, can you just please tell me how Sadie and our baby is doing?"

"Last report, the mother was in a coma and in critical condition," the female cop responded.

"What about my baby?" I asked, praying that our baby was okay.

"The fetus didn't make it," she stated coldly.

"FETUS?! HE WASN'T NO FUCKIN' FETUS!" I said as I stood up and banged on the table as I glared at that bitch. "HE WAS OUR SON!" I knew that those pigs could cuff me up or even fuck me up, but at that moment, I didn't give a shit. They had just told me that my son was dead in such a manner that made me snap. They might as well have said pass the fuckin' juice.

"Sit yo ass down!" the male cop commanded, getting all up in my damn face. Because I didn't want no problems, I just sat in the chair as calmly as I possibly could.

Getting right down to business, the male cop looked in the folder that he was holding in his hand. "I need to know what happened when you were at the victim's house earlier today."

"Look, that was way earlier! I have an alibi for where I was after that. Her name is Jackie and she can vouch for where I've been. I was over at Sadie's earlier, but we didn't argue!"

"The neighbors said there was screaming coming from the apartment," the female cop added.

"We were fuckin'! She was screaming because I was fuckin' her brains out!" I enlightened. "When I left her apartment, she was fine, and we talked after that. You can check my cell!" I insisted ready to lay it on thick as I gave the woman Jackie's number. "The only other dude I knew Sadie was messing with is De'vonte. On the streets they call him 'Brick'."

The woman's eyes lit up like she knew the nigga personally. She didn't even say shit else. She just closed her folder and got up to leave. I didn't know if that was a good or bad thing for me.

I didn't find that answer out until three hours later. That was when the female cop came back in to interrogate me some more. This time, she didn't ask one single question about Sadie's case. All she wanted to know was if I had any other information on De'vonte. I didn't know much, but I was a nigga with a great imagination. I came up with some off the wall bullshit that would have them hemming his ass up before daylight. I knew the charges wouldn't stick, but it was enough to shake his sorry ass up for a minute. Compliments of yours truly!

Chapter Ten

De'vonte

"Yes, ooooohhhh! Yessssss!" Amerika yelled out as I dug into the tight stash between her legs while I held them up in the air. As I clinched tightly onto the back of her thighs, I stared intensely into her eyes. The visual lock didn't stray until I nutted in her about a minute later.

"Damn, I love you girl," I chanted without a thought beforehand.

"You do, do you?" she giggled and embraced me.

"Yeah, you mine, right?"

"Yeah, and you all mine, right?" she repeated, stealing a kiss.

"You already know Amerika," I reminded as I felt my dick rise the moment she kissed my neck.

As her tongue swirled around to my ear, my stiffness began to pulse. I needed some head and refused to request it. Instead, I laced my fingers into Amerika's locks and gently pushed her head downward. Without hesitation, my girl licked me along my rock-hard abs until her mouth greeted the head of my dick. She opened up and welcomed him inside the warmth of her oral canal.

As the suction power became more forceful, my toes began to curl, and the speed of my thrusts increased. Before I knew it, I was ready to shoot my load.

BOOM!

Suddenly, I heard the door being kicked off the hinges. My reflexes caused me to knock Amerika back and shove her to the floor before covering her up with the blanket. Just as I was going for my weapon under the mattress, ten to twelve cops busted into my bedroom with guns drawn.

I raised my hands in confidence because I had never kept any illegal substances or firearms where I laid my head. I wasn't stupid. Looking down, I realized that I was butt ass naked and my dick was still stiff. The familiar female cop that stepped in front of all the others noticed it too.

Licking her lips, she approached me smoothly and reintroduced herself. "I'm Sergeant Cheryl Acosta."

Like clockwork, Amerika popped up soon as she heard the chick's sensual introduction. The sound of guns cocking rang through the air as the officers aimed their weapons at Amerika.

"Oh, were we interrupting something?" Cheryl Acosta teased with an added smirk.

"De'vonte! Cover up!" Amerika insisted with a disgusted look on her face as she threw me the sheet.

The sergeant's eyes stayed glued to my dick that was just starting to go limp as it relaxed on my thigh. Yeah, all ten inches of it.

"What the hell is this all about and please tell me y'all got a search warrant! Busting in people's houses and shit! Y'all better have a fuckin' warrant!" I huffed, securing the sheet around my bottom half.

"A search warrant as well as an arrest warrant for the rape and attempted murder of Sadie…"

When I heard that name, I could've flipped my damn script after discovering that the partially prepaid job wasn't completed. *That nigga didn't kill her?*

Worry traced my spine as I realized that shit could come back and bite me in the ass. I had to do something to get out of the predicament, at least until I could take care of it properly.

"When did it happen?" Amerika blurted out ready to save a nigga. "De'vonte has been here with me all day."

"Good try lil lady." Sergeant Acosta stared Amerika up and down like she had shitted on her. I wanted to check her ass, but we had a lil history. I had to get her alone to see where her head was before I started showing my ass.

"Officer Young and Officer Mays, can you please escort this woman to the other room before I have a word privately with Mr. Alexander?"

Quickly obeying, the cops had the room cleared in seconds, leaving me there in a vulnerable position. "So, we meet again huh?"

"Don't trip off the past. That was a long time ago Cheryl…"

"And you're still up to the same old shit! I should just march yo ass downtown, lock you up and throw away the damn key!" Cheryl whispered loudly shaking her finger in my face.

"What good will that do?"

"It will lock that community dick of yours up until you stop whoring around!"

"You act like you still want it?" I teased, knowing just how to get to her good side.

"That's neither here or there!"

"So, you know I ain't did no shit like they said…"

"I know you didn't, but now that I had to go through all this shit just to see your face again and see what you were up to, I have to at least take you down. Don't worry though, we'll let you right out. Now, put some clothes on so we can get the hell outta here!"

I quickly scampered around the damn room as I tried to throw on some clothes. Being the nigga that I was in these streets, I couldn't just mismatch my shit. Jail or no jail, I couldn't be caught slipping when it came to my swag. After about five minutes, I was dressed and ready to go.

Taking in a deep sigh, I held out my wrists for her to cuff me. That bitch Cheryl got all up on me, brushing her hands against my dick bringing it right back to attention. Shit, I thought she was about to drop and bless me with some bomb ass head, but instead, she led me right out to where Amerika was standing with my dick standing tall beneath my jeans. I couldn't even adjust it or cover it up because my hands were now cuffed behind me.

I watched helplessly as Amerika's saddened eyes traveled down to my erect shaft. I couldn't even face her…

Shaking her head in disgust, Amerika ran to the room and threw her clothes on. She was so mad that she beat us outside. By the time I was being shoved out the door, she was peeling out my drive-around.

"I guess she big mad, huh?" Sergeant Cheryl teased in a whisper as she made sure to put me in the back of her squad car. I guess she wanted to be my personal escort, so she could tease me all the way to the station with her nasty talk.

Honestly, I hadn't seen or thought about Cheryl in over four years. That was when she first transferred from Phoenix and got on the force in Houston. She had helped me out of many jams, but for some reason, this felt different.

As we rode down to the station, I noticed a picture of a little girl on her dash. It was a beautiful child with a familiar face. "Damn, you got a kid?"

"Yeah, she's three."

"Who's her daddy? She looks really familiar."

"She should…"

My stomach dropped at just the thought. "Stop playing with me Cheryl."

Stopping the car so hard and fast that the tires screeched, Cheryl put the gear in park and spun her head around at me. "You think I'm lying?"

"What?" I gasped still in shock. "If that baby girl was mine, you would've told me a long time ago. I ain't that damn stupid!"

"The only reason I haven't told you is because the feds have been trying to get you for the last three years! I couldn't expose something like that once I found that shit out!"

"So why tell me now?" I asked, trying to see if she was attempting to play me.

"Because now I have somebody else to pin all the shit on to throw the department off you!" Cheryl sang sneakily.

"Who?" I asked with my ears ringing.

"Sadie's baby daddy... Jordan!"

Silence came over me as I went over everything Cheryl told me. It was all a lot for me to digest, but at the end of the day, I needed my freedom. So, deciding to keep everything nice and calm until I had the cops off my back, I went down to the station, answered the questions and had Alondra pick me up. There was no way I was ready to deal with Amerika after what I had just found out.

Chapter Eleven

Alondra

"Now you wanna get your ass locked up and call me?" I fussed ready to knock De'vonte in the head. "Where's Javion?"

"He's at basketball camp!" he snapped back putting on his seatbelt as I hit the block doing 40.

"Oh yeah!" I remarked then started grilling him about why the hell he was locked up.

"Somebody raped and shot Sadie's dumb ass…"

"What?!"

"You heard me?"

"So, what the hell does that have to do with yo ass?!" I asked. I swear, if I found out that bitch was fuckin' my first child's dad too, I was going to kill her if she wasn't already dead.

"I don't fuckin' know! From what I understand, yo boy threw my name into the ring!" I said angrily.

"What are you talking about, De'vonte? Why the fuck they hem you up for the shit De'vonte?! Please don't tell me you weren't fuckin' that nasty ass scum bucket bitch!?"

"HELL NAW! I just fuckin' told you that yo baby daddy tried to hem me up! You don't listen fa shit! That's why we ain't together no mo!" he had the nerve to say.

"No, we ain't together no more because you can't keep your dick in your pants!" I reminded. "If you gonna try to point the finger at somebody, point it at the right person… your damn self!" *Now, he done pissed me the hell off.*

"Yea, whatever!" De'vonte said sucking his teeth.

"Why would Jordan point the finger at you? Why would he say that you was fuckin' Sadie if you weren't?" I asked curiously ready to catch his ass in another lie.

"How the fuck am I supposed to know why yo man do the shit he do? That nigga been sticking his fuckin' nose in ma shit! I'ma have to fix his ass!" De'vonte threatened on the low, but I caught that shit.

"What you plan on doing?"

"As if I'd tell you," he said with attitude.

"What's that supposed to mean?"

I felt somewhat offended that he would come at me like that. I had always had De'vonte's back, even when he treated me like shit and didn't have mine. I had always been loyal to him because no matter who *we* fucked with, I still loved him. He was and would always be my first love. I had loved that man for the past 14 years, ever since we were teenagers. I met De'vonte when I was only 18, but we didn't get involved until almost a year later. We had fucked, fussed, fought, cheated on each other and given each other STDs, but I still loved his dirty draws.

If he still wanted to fuck me, I wouldn't hesitate to drop my draws. I loved De'vonte and even though I was pregnant with Jordan's kid, that didn't mean anything. My loyalty would always lie with Javion's dad because my heart would always belong to him.

"Ain't you pregnant by that nigga Jordan?" De'vonte shouted out shaking me from my love spell.

"So? And what?" I asked nonchalantly.

"Just watch the fuckin' road and take me to my crib! Them fucka's done broke a nigga door down and shit!" he fumed. He pulled his phone out of his pocket and hit a button.

"Aye, I need y'all to get to my crib and replace my fuckin' front door ASAP!" he barked.

There was a pause and then he started talking again. "Them fuckin' po po's busted in my crib behind some bullshit! I need that door fixed by the time I get there." Pause. "In about 30 minutes!" Pause. "Yea." He ended the call.

"You do know that ain't nobody finna try to get caught up in yo shit, right. You got that shit like Fort Knox! A nigga would be a damn fool to break in yo shit," I said in an effort to try and ease his mind.

"It wouldn't be breaking in if the door already off the hinges, ass!"

"You ain't gotta talk to me like that!" I said as I smacked him behind his damn head. "I stopped what the fuck I was doing to come see about yo damn ass, so watch how you talk to me!"

"Keep yo fuckin' hands to yo'self, Alondra! I'm not in the fuckin' mood!"

"I ain't in the fuckin' mood either!" I huffed turning my attention back to the road. "Why didn't you call yo bitch to pick you up if you knew you was just gonna act the fool with me?"

"Shut the fuck up Alondra, DAMN!" he yelled at me. I wondered if he caught sight that he was riding in my damn car. I sho' reminded him.

"You are in my damn car! I'm not gon' tell you again to watch yo damn tone!" I snapped.

"I talk how I wanna fuckin' talk! This my fuckin' mouth and I ain't yo fuckin' kid! You can talk to that other nigga like that, but I ain't the fuckin' one!" he growled at me.

I decided to let him have that one because he clearly had a fuckin' attitude. The last thing I wanted was for us to be arguing when I was as horny as I was. I hadn't fucked nothing in a good minute.

To be brutally honest, my pussy started throbbing as soon as I realized it was De'vonte on the other end of the phone saying he needed a bitch. Shit, she was still throbbing even though he was going off on me right then. I still had so much love for that man and no matter how he treated me, I'd always be there for him. I only hoped that he had calmed down enough by the time we got to his place because I was going to try and get me some dick. De'vonte hadn't been putting out since he started fucking the principal, but I needed some dick and *I needed it now*.

Pulling up in his driveway about ten minutes later, we saw that some of the dudes from his crew were there putting the door up. While he spoke to them, I got out the car and went inside the house. I was now six and a half months pregnant and uncomfortable as hell. I was hot and horny; two things a pregnant woman should never be.

After I undressed, I went to the bathroom and did a quick wash up. By the time I was done, I heard De'vonte shut the front door.

"Alondra! ALONDRA!" he yelled. "I'ma kill that fuckin'…" He walked into the bedroom and found me lying in his bed butt ass naked. His mouth dropped, and he ran his hand down his face. He reached down and picked up my clothes off the floor and began to throw them at me. "Get the hell out of my bed, get dressed and get the hell out of my house, Alondra!"

"You don't mean that, De'vonte." I got on all fours in his bed and crawled seductively over to where he stood. I reached for his shirt, but he smacked my hand away. "Please boo, I'm so horny right now. You know how much you love pregnant pussy." I laid on the bed and touched myself. I slid my fingers in my mouth and then rubbed my clit. His eyes were glazed as he watched me. "Please."

I crawled back over to him and this time when I reached for his pants, he didn't smack my hand. While I had the chance, I slid my palm in his pants and boxers and pulled out what I had been wanting. I immediately took it into my mouth before he could change his mind. "Mmmmm!" I moaned as I stroked his hardened shaft while sucking the middle of his balls where he liked it. I applied the right amount lip action to make his knees weaken. Quickening my stroke, I moved my mouth to De'vonte's inner thigh and swirled my tongue around and sucked even harder. Knowing that it was his sensitive spot, I felt his dick began to pulsate as he moaned loudly.

Finally pushing me back on the bed, De'vonte kicked his shoes off and stripped down to nothing and strapped up with a condom. Normally I would've gotten offended, but after that STD spread, I understood.

Refocusing on the meat in front of me, I opened my legs to receive him, he lifted my legs on his shoulders and plowed into my thirsty, wet pussy. I gripped his ass cheeks as he continued to drive inside me like a jackhammer. "Oh my God!" I cried out. "Yaaassss!"

Screaming to the top of my lungs as my body shook like I was having a seizure, I held on to De'vonte for dear life. I had needed that orgasm so bad and who better to give it to me than my baby daddy? *Yes, he owned the best dick I had ever had.*

As De'vonte picked up the pace, I became delirious with all the wonderful feelings inside my mind and body. I hadn't felt this way for a couple of months and damn, a bitch felt really good right then. If he didn't get his, it wouldn't matter to me one bit because I had gotten mine like four times already.

Suddenly turning me to my side, De'vonte continued driving his anaconda inside of my honeypot. "Oh my God! Oh my God!" I cried out.

"Ain't that what you wanted?" he asked as I tried to push him back.

"Ooouuuu!" I moaned. That boy was whipping the shit out of my pussy and I was starting to feel it in my guts.

Ignoring my cries, De'vonte kept drilling inside me until he finally succumbed to the pressures of his dick. He moaned loudly before his body began to shake uncontrollably. He finally pulled out and rushed to the bathroom. I had collapsed on the bed and was getting ready to close my eyes for a long ass nap that was deeply deserved.

"Get out!" De'vonte shouted so loud that my body jumped.

"Huh?" I asked, thinking he couldn't be serious. He had worn me the hell out. I couldn't drive even if I wanted to, which I didn't.

"You heard me, Alondra! Put yo draws on and yo clothes. Slide yo ashy feet in those dingy flip flops and get the hell out!" he repeated.

"De'vonte, I'm a little worn out. Can I take a nap?"

"Yes, the hell you can! At yo own fuckin' house!" He rushed around to the side of the bed where I was laying comfortably and started tugging after my arm.

"What are you doing?" I asked in a panic as his phone began to ring.

"I'm getting you the hell out of my house!"

"Damn! You gon' just use me like that, huh? Ain't you gonna answer your phone?" I questioned trying to buy me some time. I could barely stand up.

"GET OUT OF MY HOUSE!" he demanded in an elevated tone showing me he wasn't playing.

"FINE!" I finally huffed getting out of his bed, beginning to put my clothes on. "You have ugly fuckin' ways!"

"What the fuck ever! Just get the hell outta my house!" he repeated for the tenth damn time.

"You must not want your bitch to find out about us!" I hissed.

"She ain't gonna find out shit… I know that for a fact!"

The look he gave me let me know that he wasn't playing no games with my ass. I quickly got my clothes and shoes on and rushed out the door before he could threaten me again. I hopped in my car and took off to my place. No matter how mad De'vonte was, I was happy because I had finally released what I needed to be comfortable. All six times!

Thanks for the sex boo…

Chapter Twelve

Amerika

"I know he's out!" I huffed after dialing De'vonte for the past hour. I had already found out that he was released, so I couldn't understand why he wasn't answering his damn phone.

He probably thinks I'm tripping off how he came out the room with Sergeant Acosta, with his dick still at attention.

Well I was! The woman of authority was a hot Latina, who just happened to have the face of a beauty queen and a body like a stripper. Even in that uniform, her curves could be spotted from a block away. She had to have some African American in her DNA.

I wonder what type of history they have…

The questions continued to pop in my head as I dialed De'vonte up again. When he finally answered, it caught me off guard.

"Hey," he chanted like he was out of breath.

"Did I catch you at a bad time?"

"Ah, no, I just got home and had to shower right quick. I was about to call you once I got my clothes on," he continued on while panting the whole time, causing me to feel a little insecure.

"Okay call me back when…"

"No, I can talk now. Wassup?"

"You want me to come over?" I suggested, trying to see how he was going to answer.

"No," he answered too quickly for my taste which immediately sent a red flag up. "I need to make a run right quick. How about I just come over there? Is that cool?"

"Yeah, I'll see you when you get here," I simply replied before hanging up.

I was already in too deep with De'vonte. He had won my heart, leaving me helpless when it came to staying angry with him.

Showing understanding that loving someone like De'vonte was something new to me. I was learning that I needed to start using a different approach. In order to obtain the crown, I was going to have to earn it.

Now, I was determined to be his queen, even if that meant breaking my own rules. I was going to start with cooking my man a good meal and be ready with a listening ear if he needed to talk. *And a warm pussy if he needs to fuck...*

As I prepared for De'vonte's visit, I threw some chicken on the indoor grill, placed some fresh seasoned veggies in a pot, then ran through the shower. Afterwards, I slid into something comfortable, but sexy and finished up my meal.

Just as I was opening up a chilled bottle of Stella Rosa Pink, my cell rang. When I looked at the screen, I became immediately concerned. It was Javion who was away at basketball camp.

"Is everything okay?"

"Yeah Miss Parker," he spoke quietly where I could barely hear him. "I just wanted to talk to you about Melinda."

The fact that he called me for advice truly touched me. I sat there on the phone and listened as Javion told me all about their relationship.

"Miss Parker, I don't wanna ghetto girlfriend like that. After dad talked to me about not messing around with loose girls like that and told me to get a nice girl like you..."

"Huh?" I blurted out then caught myself.

"Yeah, my dad really likes you, Miss Parker. Please don't let my mom run you off like she does with everyone else."

I knew Javion meant well, but when he said, 'everyone else', that shit touched a nerve. Made me think that Alondra had run off dozens of women! Not me though!

"I really like him too," I quickly retorted before he began asking too many questions. "Everything will work out. Don't you worry. Just tell Melinda you want to be strictly friends."

"Then she's gonna try to clown me at school!"

"About what Javion?"

"About, ah, about..."

"What does she have to clown you about Javion?" I asked more sternly, pressing him to answer.

"Please don't tell my dad," he pleaded before revealing his embarrassing ordeal.

"If it's harmless, I promise not to tell. But if it's something that's going to come back and bite you, I may have to talk with your dad, Javion."

"No, well, I don't think so," he answered, unsure of himself.

"What is it?"

"Melinda is gonna tell everyone I came fast when we did it!" he whispered loudly.

Dropping the phone, I covered my mouth to stop from screaming. It was funny and then again it wasn't. I had to put my pettiness away and be an adult.

"Javion don't worry about it. As a matter of fact, tell her she should take it as a compliment," I blurted out and immediately wanted to take it back.

"Why should she take it like that?" Javion questioned with pure innocence in his voice, but I knew better. He was the son of De'vonte.

"You know what I mean boy, stop playing!"

Javion busted out laughing. "I know, I just wanted to see what you would say!"

"I'm gonna get you when I see you!"

"Well, come with dad when he picks me up. He has a surprise for you! Don't tell him I told you though!"

"I won't and that's him at the door now," I said as I listened to the doorbell chime over and over. "You be good, and I'll see you soon."

"I will and thanks Miss Parker!"

"You're a mess, but you're welcome Javion!"

Laughing as I hung up, I went to let De'vonte in. He was dressed in sweats and a T-shirt but still handsome as ever. Just the sight of him drew me to him for a kiss.

"Mmmmmm," he hummed as he lifted me off my feet, turned in a semi-circle then gently lowered my body until my bare feet landed on the plush carpet. "You know you bring out the beast in me, right?"

"Do I?" I questioned, thinking to myself... *Just like that Sergeant Acosta did when she sent you out the room with a stiff dick?!*

I didn't blurt it though. I kept it cool and fed him some delicious food, listened to his complaints about being arrested then was ready to go to the bedroom. After grabbing the fifth of Tequila De'vonte had been sipping on since he got there, I followed right behind him.

He was now loaded up with alcohol, so I was hoping that he was ready to spill the beans. *You know, a drunk mind speaks with a sober tongue!*

"So, how did you say you got home from the station?" I questioned as I watched him removing his clothes.

"I used my Uber app. I didn't want you to have to come and get me, especially after the way you looked at me when I left."

"I was just tripping off your dick being hard still..." I whispered as I touched his manhood through his blue plaid boxers. "Just like it is now."

"You know you have that effect on me."

De'vonte was saying all the right things, and when he began touching all the right spots, I forgot all about the interrogation that I had all planned out. At that moment, all I could think about was being intimate with my man.

Taking the lead, De'vonte serviced me first and brought on two quick orgasms from my still quivering body. Once he figured I was satisfied, he reversed it so that we were in the 69 position, with him on top. While he fucked my face, he dug his tongue deeply inside me making me lift my wide hips up in the air. As our thrusts became rhythmic, we both exploded together.

Trying not to gag, I eased De'vonte over and choked silently into the sheet. As I lifted up, he was behind me trying to enter me from the rear. Struggling to get up on my knees, he snatched me upwards and plunged inside me over and over again.

"Amerika…"

The sound of my name ringing from De'vonte's mouth had me delirious. He had taken my mind and my body to another world and I was enjoying the trip.

"Ahhhhh!" I shouted out as he unexpectedly flipped me onto my back and entered right back inside of me. Now, he was staring down at me as he gave me his all. Our eyes locked immediately, and we released again, together.

"Amerika, baby damn. I love you girl."

My heart fluttered faster and harder than it ever had. That was it. De'vonte had me gone…

Chapter Thirteen

De'vonte

After waking up to Amerika with a smile on her face the next morning, I knew that she had felt what I gave her and told her. I meant that shit too. I was ready to make her mine, just as soon as I wrapped up all the other bullshit that was going on in my life.

Creeping up out the bed to get my cell, I slid into my boxers and grabbed it off the floor. It had been vibrating all night until the battery went dead.

I plugged it in as I got in the shower to wait for it to automatically power back on. When I got out, the light on it was flashing.

Unlocking my phone, I discovered that it was Cheryl calling and texting me. Knowing that the situation with her was very private, I went ahead and got dressed and dipped out without disturbing Amerika.

Soon as I got in my car, I dialed Cheryl back without checking her text messages. "What's up?"

"I just wanna let you know, I'm on your case and we should have it taken care of soon."

I could hear a trembling in her voice, so I questioned her about it. "Is everything okay? You don't sound like yourself right now." As the line grew quiet, I put Cheryl on speaker and read her messages. She was in her feelings and if her daughter was mine, I understood why.

"After all this shit is behind us, we are gonna take the DNA test and…"

"You must not have looked at the last picture text," she whispered into the phone, sending me to check my inbox again.

"How the hell did you do that?"

"Remember when I arrested you? I got your pubic hair and a toothbrush," she revealed. "I had the results rushed back through the lab. If you're questioning them, we can go together to take another one."

My stomach sank as the reality of having another child hit me. This wasn't an infant we were referring to! This beautiful little girl was three-years-old! Walking and talking and everything! This whole thing had a nigga shook.

"I know it's a lot to take in, and like you said, after all this is over, we will discuss everything," Cheryl added. "I'm here with Amaya now…"

"That's her name?" I gasped, knowing she was named after my mother.

"Yeah, I know how close you used to be with her…" Cheryl's words trailed off. "I'll just call you back. She's right here jumping all over me."

"Mommy, mommy, who are you talking to?"

The little girl's voice was sweet enough for me to fall for. I had to go. I couldn't deal with it right then.

"Okay, call me back."

Hanging up without waiting for a response, I sat my phone down and thought about Javion. He was my firstborn, making him the leader of all my seeds to come. I needed to get him straight, so he could set a good example for Amaya. Whenever I got up enough nerve to tell him about her.

Damn, I have a daughter! A lil girl!

Dialing up Javion, I checked to see what time I was supposed to be picking him up later on that evening. He answered on the first ring.

"Hey dad! I'm glad you called!"

"Oh yeah? Why's that?"

"Because you need to bring Miss Parker with you when you come get me."

"Huh?"

"Dad just listen, okay. Bring her with you and have a surprise for her."

"Boy, what the hell are you talking about?"

"Just trust me dad! Bring her and have a surprise for her! Now, I gotta go but I'll be at the Boys and Girls Club at seven tonight."

Javion hung up on me, leaving me speechless. That lil boy had gone and set a nigga up to do some shit that I was not prepared to do! Now I had to come up with a romantic plan. Something I wasn't too good at.

As I sat in my truck, I thought about the fact that I had a daughter now. That was going to take some getting used to; first I had a teenage son and now, I had a three-year old daughter. That shit was definitely some crazy shit and it was going to take some getting used to. I had to figure out how to break the news to not only my son, but my woman as well. I knew that Amerika loved my son. They got along great, but how would she react to me having another kid? Hell, I didn't even know that Cheryl was pregnant by me.

I understood the reasons behind her not telling me that I had a daughter. I wouldn't want anything to happen to that precious little girl with her mother's line of work and my street life as well.

Cheryl was a hell of a cop, so I knew with her on my case, that shit would work out in my favor. I didn't know what I'd do without her, especially knowing that the feds were trying to lock me up on some trumped-up charges. Even though I ordered Sadie to be killed, I never ordered her to be raped. That nigga I hired had some explaining to do.

Hitting Jake up, I let him know that I needed to see his ass. He had been blowing up my damn phone for the rest of the payment on the job he did, but little did he know that he wasn't getting the whole 10 G's. I mean, that nigga had added rape to the list. All I asked him to do was kill the bitch. *Why the fuck would he rape a pregnant woman? Nigga gon' fuck around and have his dick fall off fucking that dirty bitch.*

"Aye, Brick!" he answered, sounding on top of the world.

"Jake, where you at nigga?"

"I'm actually just leaving my crib," he said.

"Stay put! I'm on my way!"

"You got my money?"

"Stay put, muthafucka!" I spat before ending the call.

I didn't have time to play with that nigga and he knew the kind of nigga that I was. Why would he do some shit I didn't ask him to do? He was supposed to go in, shoot her ass, and get the fuck out… simple shit!

Pulling up to his crib half an hour later, I hopped out of the truck. As soon as I walked up to the door, it flew open. "Waddup Block?!" the nigga was smiling like a Cheshire cat that had ate the last goldfish in the bowl.

I walked in and soon as he shut the door, I went in on him. "What the fuck is wrong with you, nigga?!" I questioned eyeing him down angrily.

"Whatchu talkin' bout?" His face showed the level of confusion his brain was experiencing.

"What'd I ask you to do?" I repeated through clinched teeth trying to control the level of my tone. "What the fuck did I ask you to do?"

"You asked me to kill that chick! I did what you asked!"

"Did you muthafucka?"

"Hell yea, I did! I don't know who you been talking to, but I did exactly what you asked me to do!"

"Nigga, if you had done exactly what I asked, I would've thanked you, gave you the rest of the dough and left. THE BITCH IS STILL ALIVE NIGGA!"

"Say WHAT?"

"You heard me… she's still alive! Not only that, but the fuckin' cops tried to hem me up for the job!" I enlightened his dumb ass.

"I swear I thought that bitch was dead, Block! I shot that ho' in her fuckin' head!" he explained nervously.

"Well, I'on know where you shot her, but the bitch still breathing!" I said. "So, tell me this… why you raped that ho'? Ain't you see she was pregnant?"

"I ain't raped that girl!"

"The police said the bitch was raped. They tried to get me to say I did that shit. What the fuck is wrong with you, nigga? You have one simple fuckin' job to do… shoot the bitch and leave! You couldn't even do that!" I fussed.

"How was I supposed to know that she wasn't dead?"

"Uh, you ever heard of a pulse, nigga?! If hers still beating, she ain't dead!" I continued.

"Sorry about that, but uh…" The nigga looked around nervously as if he were scared to look at me. "Can I get them 10 G's you promised me?"

"FUCK NO! Do I look like a fool to you?"

"Whatchu mean?"

"I offered you some serious ends to rock a bitch to sleep. You didn't do it! I ain't fuckin' paying you for that shit!"

"You're kidding, right? I mean, I shot that bitch! How the fuck was I supposed to know she was fuckin' Superwoman?"

"I ain't giving you another fuckin' dime!" I said in a sterner tone.

"WHAT?!"

"Did I stutter, muthafucka? I ain't payin' you one more, red cent for not completing a job I signed you up to do!"

"Aw, fuck that! You gon' pay me my money!"

I looked around the place because I knew somebody else had to be in the room. That nigga couldn't have been popping off on me like that. He definitely had me fucked all the way up. It didn't seem like he knew how to complete a job, but I had something for his ass.

"Nigga, who the fuck you talkin' to like that?"

"Aye Block, I was counting on that bread fa something, yo! I need my bread!"

"What you need to do is back the fuck up..."

"Or what?' he asked as he stepped closer.

"Jake, you already know how I get down in the streets..."

"We ain't in the streets. This shit is between us. I want my fuckin' mo..."

POW!

Before he had a chance to say another fuckin' word, I reached in my waistband, pulled out my nine and shot that nigga dead in the stomach. I didn't know who the fuck he thought he was playing with like that, but I wasn't the one.

He fell to the floor screaming like a bitch. "YOU SHOT ME!" he cried.

"Fuckin' right I shot yo ass. You act like you don't know how to speak to a real one when you see one." I bent down to his level and said, "You didn't know how to kill a bitch, so lemme show you!"

"BRICK, I'M SO…"

POW!

Blew a bullet straight between that muthafucka's eyes. *He gon' understand how shit worked in the hood now.* I walked out that nigga's spot like it wasn't shit. Thankfully, that fool lived in the hood. Hood rules always applied; *you didn't see shit unless it was yo shit.*

Hopping in my truck, I headed over to pick up Amerika. I decided to take my son's advice and bring her with me to pick him up.

Chapter Fourteen

Alondra

I hadn't seen De'vonte in a week. Last time I saw him, he was throwing me out of his house like I was yesterday's trash. He wanted to act like we didn't have sex, but we did. I wondered if he told his school bitch that we fucked. Knowing him, I bet he hadn't.

Now they were over there playing happy lil home with *my son*, who had just come back from basketball camp last week. I had yet to see him. I missed Javion and now that Jordan was out of the picture, I saw no reason why my son couldn't move back home with me.

I decided that I was going to head over to De'vonte's house to speak with him about that. I knew that Javion was enjoying his time with his dad but considering everything that happened between him and that lil hot ass girl, I thought he should return home where I could keep an eye on him. Spring break was in a couple of weeks so that would be the perfect time to get my son back in the house where he belonged. Don't get me wrong, I was happy that De'vonte had stepped up to take care of our son. Most dudes from the hood didn't take care of their seeds, but De'vonte always took care of our son and I never had to beg him or nothing.

From day one when I told him I was pregnant, he stepped up as a dad. I loved the way that De'vonte behaved around my son, *our son*. I wished I could say the same about Jordan, but I could already see that I was going to have to put that nigga on child support because he wasn't gonna act right. As it was, I hadn't seen him in almost a month. I was done with him anyway, so he never had to come over here. I'd just serve his dumb ass with child support papers. Whether he had a legit job or a street job, I didn't give two fucks because our kid came first.

Grabbing my keys and purse, I headed for the door. Why as soon as I opened the door, Jordan was standing on my doorstep getting ready to knock? By this time, I was in the middle of my third trimester, so the last thing I wanted from him was sex or an argument.

Staring directly at him with a raised brow, I said, "I don't know why you're here, but I'm on my way out."

"I need your help," he muttered, brushing past me.

I rolled my eyes and closed the door behind him. "Whatever it is, I'm not interested."

"I really need your help Alondra."

"You need my help with what, Jordan?" I asked.

"I need an alibi, man."

"An alibi? For what?"

"Sadie got hurt and they think I did it," Jordan sang out with anxiousness in his voice.

"What happened to that bitch?" I asked, even though I really didn't give a damn.

"Somebody shot her."

"What?!" I asked in surprise because that was news to me.

"Yea, somebody shot her and she's in a coma, so now them cops trying to pin that shit on me, but I didn't do it."

"Wow! I didn't know that shit. So why you need me to alibi you? You weren't even here with me! As a matter of fact, I haven't been seeing you for a while now. I don't even know why you here now!" I spat sarcastically.

"The alibi I got ain't coming through, so I need someone else to vouch for me. I can't go down for no shit I didn't do," he said.

"I'm not finna do that."

Shit, I didn't have to think about if I was gon' do it or not. I wasn't doing shit for Jordan's ass. That nigga had beat me, raped me, cheated on me, slammed me with STDs... *whatever happens to him let it happen.*

I was out of that and wasn't about to lie to the police to get him off. Whether he was involved with what happened to the Sadie bitch had nothing to do with me.

"Are you fuckin' serious right now?" he asked, shock evident on his face.

"I'm dead serious. Whatever is going on with you has nothing to do with me. I don't want to be involved... at all."

"Alondra, please. You want me to be locked up when you have our baby?"

"When I have my baby..."

"OUR BABY! I done lost one kid already, I'm not about to lose another one!" he cried snatching my attention.

"What?"

"Sadie lost the baby," he said with tears in his eyes.

"I'm sorry. I didn't know."

"Yea. So, you see, I can't lose this baby too."

Looking at him, I almost felt sorry for him, but after everything we had been through, fuck that!

"Look Jordan, I'm sorry about everything that you're going through. I really am, but I'm not going to give you an alibi."

"Woooow! You so foul for that shit! If it was that nigga De'vonte, you wouldn't hesitate to say that muthafucka was with you!"

"You can't compare yourself to my other baby daddy. We have way too much history."

"So, it's just fuck me, huh?" he asked.

"You said it."

"Well, you know what Alondra… FUCK YOU! FUCK YOU AND YOUR UGLY ASS MUTHAFUCKIN' BABY DADDY!" he said as he headed towards the front door.

"FUCK YOU TOO, JORDAN! I've done way too much for you to have you treating me like this!"

"FUCK YOU!" he said as he walked toward the door.

"Ugh, I swear! I hate yo ass!" I blurted out trying to close him on the other side.

"You know what?" Jordan hollered and shoved me backwards into the house. "I hate yo ass too!"

Grabbing me by the neck, that nigga snatched me up so fast and pinned me against the wall so hard that my head was hurting. Nigga had me all delusional and shit. In fear that he was about to harm me or my baby, I tried to calm him down.

Opening my mouth, nothing came out. All I could do was plead with my eyes by allowing the tears to fall.

"Why the fuck should I let you live right now Alondra? I don't have shit to lose! I got a case hanging over my head that ain't had shit to do with me! I lost my seed! Now yo bitch ass is supposed to have my back and you wanna see a nigga locked up? Fuck you and that baby!"

I became lightheaded as a knocking came at the door. I wasn't expecting nobody, but God sent somebody to help me.

"I should just snap yo fuckin' neck!" Jordan threatened in a whisper.

Gaining up just enough strength to try and save my life, I took my knee and lifted it as high and hard as I could. I dropped to the floor, but still couldn't get the breath out to scream.

Jordan reared his foot back to kick me and instead of shielding my stomach, I clinched onto his ankle and caught him off guard. He quickly lost his balance and fell into the table, knocking it over along with all the ceramic elephants I had on there.

"Mom!" I heard Javion holler from the other side of the door. I sure didn't want him to see what was going on in here, but it was too late. He had already used his key to come in, De'vonte and Amerika were standing right by his side as they took in the scene before them.

"He tried to kill me!" I forced my words out just as Jordan peeled himself off the floor and jetted out the front door. De'vonte's reactions were delayed because he was too busy holding hands with that Amerika bitch to try to stop him.

"What happened mom? Are you okay?" Javion questioned with worry as he rushed to help me up with the assistance of Amerika. I snatched away from her and shot her a frown then smiled at my son.

My stomach was starting to cramp, but I ignored the pain to shield Javion. "I'm fine, now."

"Glad we came by when we did!" Amerika huffed while going back to hold onto De'vonte's arm. That bitch had a lot of nerve even being in my house.

"Thanks, but why are you guys here?"

"I was coming to get some of my stuff. I needed some help to carry it out," Javion explained as he rushed off to his room.

"You cool?" De'vonte asked, not really looking concerned in the least. I bet if that shit had happened to his new bitch, he would've been all over a nigga. I wondered when his feelings for me got so unbothered and to the point where he didn't give two shits about me; at least that was how it looked to me.

"I'm straight. That nigga gon' get his."

"Yeah, he sho' is! Cops already after him about that Sadie shit."

"So, you knew?"

"Yeah, they tried to hem me up for that shit too."

I didn't give a damn about all that shit! What about what I was going through? That nigga Jordan almost killed me and there stood my other baby daddy, the only one I really cared about, in my damn house with his new bitch. I was too through!

"Whatever De'vonte! Just help get Javion's shit and get out!" I shouted ready to cry about everything that happened. I had never felt so alone in my life. It was like no one even cared. I ran off and shut myself in my room.

Now, I really didn't want to talk to De'vonte about Javion coming back to live with me. I wasn't about to risk being embarrassed again. I knew my son wasn't ready to come back home…

Chapter Fifteen

Amerika

I really didn't think it was a good idea to go with De'vonte and Javion to his mother's house. I knew how she felt about me, but when they insisted they needed help getting his bike and some containers, I agreed.

Why did I do that?

Alondra was rude just like always! I was trying to help her ass up off the damn floor after her boyfriend almost choked the life out of her! Evidently, she wasn't that hurt to brush me off the way that she did. Well, fuck her!

"I'm sorry she always gotta act like that," De'vonte apologized when we got back to his house.

Heading to the kitchen, I prepared dinner while we chatted. Before long, Javion had joined us.

"I like eating like this," he said, shoving a big spoonful of garlic and butter mashed potatoes in his mouth.

"Oh, so you like my cooking?" I giggled before taking another gulp of my red wine.

"I mean the three of us eating dinner together like this," Javion clarified while still feeding his face. "You cook good too though."

Looking over at De'vonte, I saw an expression full of love as he stared at his son who wasn't paying him a lick of attention. He was eating like he had been starving all day long.

"Thanks Javion," I quickly replied, kicking De'vonte under the table.

"Ouch!" he yelled out then laughed when he got the hint.

"You aight dad?" Javion chuckled without glancing away from his plate.

"Yeah, but, ah, you like us all together here like this, huh?"

"It's like on the movies, you know, when the family all sits down together. Well, I know it's only us three, but I like it."

"Don't worry, we're gonna be doing it a lot more often."

"You moving in?!" Javion questioned finally giving us all his attention, even though his gaze was shooting directly at me. "That would be dope Miss Parker! Oh, and what if y'all got married?!"

"Whoa! You are getting way too far ahead of yourself Javion…" I began before De'vonte cut me off.

"Nah, he's not. Maybe one day he'll get his wish," De'vonte spoke slyly, staring me down as he licked his top lip before biting down on his bottom one. That shit got me every damn time!

"That would be the shit… I mean that would be cool!" Javion said, quickly correcting himself.

"You betta watch yo mouth, boy! You ain't too old to get knocked out!" De'vonte snapped sternly without elevating his tone one bit. It worked every time!

"I apologize dad and to you Miss Parker," he said sincerely before busting out in a grin.

"Get outta here boy!" De'vonte laughed and threw a balled-up napkin at Javion as he jetted out the kitchen without removing his plate from the table.

Once he was out of earshot, I eased around to the other side of the table and kissed my man. I really laid it on him and had him gasping.

"Shit!"

"I love you," I whispered lowly in his ear before releasing him.

Standing to his feet, De'vonte pulled me back to him and kissed me again. I could feel his dick rise on my stomach through his jeans.

As I got excited, he drew away to look down at me. "I love you too and I meant that shit about taking our relationship to the next level…"

"I'm practically over here all the time now, there's no need for me to move in, De'vonte." I repeated to him for the second time. "I don't want to move in with any man out of wedlock…"

"I told you I meant what I said. You know eventually we will probably…"

Those were too many words of doubt in one sentence for me.

"Let's not rush into anything, okay? I love what we have…"

"I love having you here and so does Javion! You heard him."

"Yes, I did, and I love being here with you guys too. I just don't want to rush into anything."

De'vonte was feeling the alcohol and he was all on me trying to convince me to move in with them. Every reason he was giving had me second guessing the rules I set for myself.

To stop him from pressing it, I reminded him of the basketball films he had to get ready for practice the following day. That kept him busy just long enough for him to make sure Javion was sleep. Then he came to find me in the den wrapping up my own paperwork.

"What's this?" he questioned, picking up the grant proposal I had drawn up to start my own charter school. I knew it was going to be a lot of work, but I was determined to help the students who seemed to fall through the cracks.

"I want to open my own charter school," I said. I had been keeping this a secret from him because I didn't think he would be interested in it. As I watched him read over the paperwork, I began to think that maybe I was wrong.

"Your own school? How long have you been planning this?"

"Uh, not that long," I lied. The truth of the matter was that I had been wanting my own school. I had wanted it since before I even met De'vonte Alexander.

"I like this, but you don't have to ask nobody for this money baby. I gotchu!" De'vonte stated as he continued to read over the documents. "This right here is a great idea! This could actually help some of the kids that got it hard!"

My heart melted at his gestures and his actual concerns for the troubled youth in our community. He was amazing me every day and I loved it.

"I need to do this for a formality though. I need all my paperwork, licenses and certifications in order before I can make this happen. I already have a team of teachers and staff ready to back me. I just can't wait to make it happen. It just seems so unreal right now," I admitted, realizing that it may take more than another year to get the appropriate authorizations and proper funding.

"I know folks and if you're serious about this shit, I can make this shit a reality for you before the next school year starts," De'vonte offered. "I've just been waiting for a business opportunity that I could be involved in personally. This shit right here is the truth, baby. You are so fuckin' smart and that shit is sexy as hell."

Dropping the stack of papers on the table, De'vonte drew me up and reminded me that Javion was sleeping. "Come on, let's talk about this in the bedroom."

Yeah, right! We ain't gonna get no talking done in there!

Laughing to myself, I followed De'vonte's lead to the master bedroom that was fit for a royal couple. We didn't even make it to the pillowtop mattress. We wound up on the white sheepskin rug that was positioned on the floor between the bottom of his bed and the fireplace.

That man never disappointed! De'vonte took his time and made sure that he made me climax until my body shook before he got his. Every time we made love, no matter how many ways, one of the positions would always include him being on top. He always had to stare at me to the point that I could feel how he was feeling. The shit was scary but touching. It made me fall for him even harder…

Without getting up, De'vonte held onto me until he drifted off with a light snore. Feeling a sticky mess, I eased from his grip and went to shower. When I came out, De'vonte's cell was going off. Usually, I wouldn't snoop, but it wouldn't stop chiming.

Letting curiosity get the best of me, I lifted his cell off the floor and touched the screen. It was locked, but I could view the messages. They were all from Alondra. She was talking shit about how De'vonte just stood there and did nothing to help her after Jordon attacked her. Then the bitch had the nerve to start talking shit about me. Calling me all types of fat bitches and homely looking ho's. That heffa even threatened to get me fired from my job! She said that she was going to send the school district a letter saying that I was going around sleeping with the student's fathers!

There had to be at least a dozen messages and I couldn't even read them all or the full text; only the beginning. That was enough for me. I had to say something.

Getting all my clothes on first, including my shoes, I grabbed my keys and woke De'vonte up. He struggled to open his eyes and drag himself to the sitting position. "Where are you going?"

"I'm going to the house. I probably shouldn't have, but I read some of the texts Alondra is steadily sending…"

Ding, Buzz, Ding, Buzz…

"Like that shit right there," I smirked and drew my blouse fully closed while listening to De'vonte's cell as it continued to go off. "I'll let you handle that. Just call me later."

"Wait, Amerika! Don't let her run you off!"

"I'm not letting her run me off. I just need to be prepared for whatever fast one she tries to pull."

"Wait, what fast one? What are you talking about?" he asked, reaching for my arm to stop me while he checked his messages.

After several seconds, he sat his phone down and looked at me. "I wish she would do some childish shit like that!"

"That's my job, De'vonte!" I screamed out ready to cry. Shit, I had never been fired from a job in my life, let alone had to deal with an embarrassing scandal like the one Alondra was trying to pin on me.

"You know how hood shit is and if this spins out of control before I can check it, I gotcha back!"

"You can't do shit about cleaning up a ruined reputation!" I shouted with tears now escaping my over filled eyes.

"I'm gonna talk to her and keep her ass at bay for these next few months while we get your school up and running. If she stirs up trouble before then, I'll handle it."

Yes, my man took charge and had me feeling a totally different way about the whole situation. I didn't have to rely on that funky VICE principal job when I could be my own boss!

"Thank you, baby," I chanted, planting a kiss on his pouty lips.

"Thank me for what?" he laughed and held me around my waist without a lick of clothes on. His dick was on the rise now.

"Thanks for having my back and making me see the other side of things. The boss side."

"Yeah, that's because you fuckin' with a boss and you about to be a boss. We about to do boss shit. Watch and see baby. Watch and see…"

Chapter Sixteen

De'vonte

Alondra's ass knew how to fuck up a wet dream! I was so sick of her interfering in my relationship with Amerika. I couldn't wait to check her after texting me like that. Soon as Amerika and Javion went out the door the next morning, I dialed her up and went in on her.

"You getting mad at me behind the next bitch when I was over here damn near dead?!" Alondra screamed loudly; enough for me to take the phone away from my ear for a few seconds.

"Yo ass was okay!"

"Yeah, but I would've been dead if you hadn't come over!"

"Well shut the fuck up and thank me for saving your life instead of threatening my woman!"

"Yo woman!? Nigga I got your fuckin' son! Your only child! Nobody else should come in front of me!"

Immediately thinking about my daughter, I bit my tongue before exposing my secret. It was the perfect time to throw it in her face, but then she wouldn't do shit but run back and tell Amerika before I had the chance. I had to chill on that one.

"Anyway, why you wanna threaten Amerika's job?" I inquired before really fucking with Alondra's head. I couldn't resist. "You know if she gets fired, I'll just take care of her, right? Pay all her bills and buy her all the shit she needs. Probably just move her in so I can..."

"Ain't nobody thinking about calling her job! I should though! Especially since she had all that fuckin' courage to come up in my house and then try to help me up?!"

"She was trying to help you Alondra! Ain't that what you said you needed? Damn, you don't know what the hell you want or need!"

"I need some more dick, so bring it over here or better yet... let me come get it. I know Javion and Big Ol' Miss Parker are gone to school by now."

"You will never get this shit again!"

"Bet I do, or yo bitch will get more humiliated than she could ever imagine at that school! That would be worth it now that I think about it!"

"I wish you would. As a matter of fact, I dare you to do it."

"You threatening me De'vonte? The mother of your only child," she cried.

"Nah, nothing like that. You know I never make idle threats to anyone. I make fuckin' promises and if I'm making a promise to you, you already know how that shit gon' turn out. I promise you that if you try and make trouble for Amerika, you ain't ever gotta look for me to do shit for you again!" I said through clenched teeth.

"What's that supposed to mean?"

"It means, when yo crappy ass get into a tight one and need some cash, don't call me. It means that when yo landlord come around asking where his rent money at, don't call me if yo ass is short. It means…"

"Alright, I get it! I don't know why you feel the need to go the extra mile for a bitch who is clearly big enough to defend her damn self. She don't need you to stand up for her big ass!" she said.

"Amerika is just my size. Maybe if you had put on a little more weight, I'd still be fuckin' with you. Sometimes, a nigga likes a lil meat on his bones, ya know? And Amerika got all the meat I…"

CLICK!

Yea, I knew that would get her dumb ass. I laughed at her so hard, I almost pissed on myself. Alondra was all talk, no bite. She could pull that shit on other people if she wanted to, but that shit didn't work with me. I already knew which buttons to press where she was concerned. The shrill ringing of my phone jerked me out of my thoughts of Alondra. I looked at the number and saw that it was Cheryl.

"Hey Cheryl."

"De'vonte, I just wanted to let you know that this thing with Jordan will be over real soon. I want to introduce you to Amaya right after. I feel that she's been deprived of her daddy long enough."

"She ain't the only one been deprived," I stated honestly.

"I know, but I explained that…"

"I know, and I understand. It's just that finding out I have a daughter and she's already three years old. I missed out on so much already, ya know?"

"I do, and I can't apologize enough."

"No, you're good. Just know that once you bring her into my life, I'm always going to be present in hers. I'm never going to miss another moment of her growing up." I assured Cheryl from my heart.

"Thank you," she said.

"For what?"

"For not being angry with me."

"Why would I be angry? I know you only did what you did to protect our daughter. I can't fault you for anything."

"Not to change the subject, but we got Sadie to point the finger at Jordan as the perpetrator," she said.

"Word? I thought she was in a coma," I said.

"She's barely clinging to life. She came to briefly and we just happened to be there. I asked her who did that to her and she said Jordan. That's enough for an arrest."

"Damn! That nigga really did it huh?"

"It looks like it," Cheryl explained. "I'll let you know when we have him in custody. We already have the warrant, but we've been having trouble locating him."

"Shit, I wished I had known sooner. He was just at my baby mama's house."

"What?! You talking about Alondra?"

"Yep."

"Are you serious?"

"Yea, the two of them have a child on the way. He tried to kill her a couple of days ago too," I informed Cheryl. Anything I could do to get that nigga locked the hell up, I was going to do it. It was kind of funny how he tried to get my ass hemmed up, but the tables turned right back around on him. Now, he was about to go down for some shit that I had put in motion. *That nigga better learn not to fuck with me.*

"Damn! Why didn't she report this to the police?" Cheryl asked.

"Because that ain't how we handle shit in the hood. You know that shit!"

"Yea, I do. What's her address?"

"Why?"

"I'm gonna have to go by her place and question her."

I gave her Alondra's address as she wrote it down. "Keep me posted," I said.

"You already know," she said.

"Aight."

"De'vonte?"

"Yea?"

"I still love you," Cheryl said.

"Cheryl…"

"I'm not looking for you to say it back. I know what happened between us was a long time ago and you're involved with someone else. I just had to let you know that I've never stopped loving you. No matter how much time passed, I could never forget about you or what we had. I mean, we have a precious little girl as a product of our past. I just wanted to let you know that," she spoke sincerely.

I felt like I should've said something back… not no 'I love you' or nothing like that, but something. I couldn't get my words to come out right. Shit, I couldn't even untie my damn tongue to try and put those words together. I had to try though.

"Cheryl, what we had was very special, but that's a part of our past. The good thing is that we do have our daughter and she'll always be a reminder of the great times we shared. Let's just keep our focus on being the best parents we can be to Amaya."

"You're right. Sorry for getting all sappy," she sniffled. I could picture her dabbing at her tears with the sleeve of her shirt like she used to. I had caused her enough hurt, and pain in the past to remember what that looked like. "I'll talk to you later."

"Yeah, be careful out there."

We ended the call and I went about my business, confident that by the end of the week Jordan's ass would be locked up.

Chapter Seventeen

Jordan

Nothing in my fucking life was going right these days. I went over to Alondra's to ask her to verify my alibi. I should've known that bitch wouldn't come through for a nigga. She couldn't wait to see me get locked up, even if I was innocent just so she could act the fool behind that loser ass Block. I didn't know how the police thought I had tried to kill Sadie. I didn't want Sadie dead and I sure as hell didn't want my seed dead. I loved that kid even though I hadn't seen the baby yet. Now, I'd never see the child born because it was killed. I didn't even know if it was a boy or a girl.

I could've asked the police when they told me about it, but the truth of the matter was that I didn't wanna know. It was only going to hurt me more to find out if I was having a son.

Then there was Alondra. When I left her house, I was disgusted with her ass. She was lucky that her bratty kid showed up at the door with his punk ass daddy when he did. Otherwise, young Javion would've been planning his mom's funeral. I was definitely ready to kill that shady bitch, with her traitor ass.

Seeing Block standing there with his new bitch made me smile though. The new bitch showing up at Alondra's place was some funny shit. I wished I could've been a fly on the wall to see that shit go down. When I jetted out of the house and saw Block's fuckin' ass, I wanted to snap on that nigga but I ain't have time. He was gonna get his in due time though.

I'd give anything to be able to take his cocky ass out and get away with it. If I thought I could pay somebody to knock him off, I would. But the way the streets worked, a murder like that wouldn't be kept under wraps.

I couldn't pull no shit like that off if I wanted to.

Taking the 'I don't give a fuck' attitude, I swung by Jackie's place. I needed to know where the fuck she was when the cops was calling to verify that I was deep in her guts that night. All I needed was for her to tell the fuckin' truth to those pigs so they could get off my damn back. Every time the cops called her for verification, she wouldn't answer. They even said they went by the house using the address I gave them, but she wasn't home. Yeah, I was very salty with her ass about that shit. I don't know why she wouldn't talk to those people for me. It wasn't like I was asking her to lie like I had asked Alondra.

Pulling up to Jackie's spot, I jumped out and knocked on her door. I saw the blinds moving in the living room, so I knew that she was in the house. "JACKIE! I KNOW YOU IN THERE! OPEN THE FUCKIN' DOOR!" I yelled.

"I AIN'T HOME!" she yelled back.

This bitch thinks I'm playing with her ass. "OPEN THE FUCKIN' DOOR BEFORE I KICK IT IN!"

"I'M CALLING THE COPS!"

BOOM! BOOM! BOOM!

I kicked that shit in and rushed up on her ass as she was dialing numbers on her phone. I yoked her up by the neck and threw her against the wall.

"BITCH YOU THINK I'M PLAYING WITH YOU!" I yelled in her face. I was so mad that when I spoke, spittle flew from my mouth into her face. All I wanted was for her to give me a solid alibi. All I wanted was for her to tell the fuckin' truth.

"Let me go!" she cried as she struggled to get away.

"All I wanna know is why haven't you spoken to the cops to verify that I was with you that night?" I asked.

"I don't know what you're talking about?" she said, her voice barely above a whisper.

"Yea, that's funny because I think you know exactly what the fuck I'm talking about!"

"Please Jordan, I really don't know."

If she was gonna play these games with me, then I thought it was time for me to let her know that I played to kill. As I squeezed harder around her neck, cutting off her oxygen, her eyes began to bulge out of her head. She scratched my hands as tears streamed from her eyes.

"You gonna tell me the truth now?" I asked.

She nodded her head affirmatively, so I dropped her. She coughed as she struggled to breathe. Once she had gotten enough air in her fuckin' lungs, I snatched her up by her fake hair. She winced as I stared into her eyes. "I wanna know why you ain't giving me a fuckin' alibi."

"I don't…"

SMACK!

I slapped the shit out of that bitch. I wasn't about to stand there and let her lie to me. "Before you claim to not know what I'm talking about, I already know that ain't true. All I want is the truth or I'm going to kill you. I ain't got shit to lose since they already accusing me of trying to kill my baby mama. If I go down for that shit, I might as well make it two for one. TALK BITCH!"

Jackie's lips trembled as she stared at me. I could tell she was afraid, but since this shit was life or death, she had every right to be scared.

"De'vonte…"

"De'vonte? What the fuck does he have to do with this shit?" I asked.

"He paid me to not give you an alibi."

"The fuck?! How you know him?"

She looked like she didn't want to tell me, but I let her know what would happen if she didn't speak. "You better keep talking because this is life or death for you," I threatened.

"I've known him for years."

The lightbulb went on in my head as I put the pieces together. That nigga had played me, and he had used this bitch to do it. As my rage began to build up in me, all I saw was red. I was about to really go to jail for murder because I was going to kill two fuckin' people.

"Before you even think about doing some crazy shit Jordan, De'vonte has a cop in his pocket and she's been having this place watched…"

"Bitch, you set me up too?"

Becoming paranoid, I rushed out of Jackie's house, looking over my shoulder the entire jog to my car that I parked at the end of the block. Luckily, I was driving a little bucket that was registered in my sister's name.

Drawing my Houston Rockets cap down low over my forehead, I hopped in the car and went to the only person that could help me; Sadie. Taking my chances, I drove to the hospital and went up to her room. There was no on outside of the door just like before.

Sneaking in, I was greeted by her mother and her little brat ass daughter, Melinda. I couldn't stand that lil bitch and was glad when she went to stay with her grandmother. I wasn't looking for any trouble with these two. All I wanted to do was see if Sadie would wake up, so she could clear my fuckin' name.

"What the fuck are you doing here?" her mom asked as she stared me down.

"Ma'am, I didn't come for any trouble. I just wanted the chance to see Sadie," I said.

"Get the hell out of here! If it wasn't for you, my mother wouldn't be in this situation!" Melinda said.

"Yo mom ain't in this shit cuz of me! I didn't do this to her!" I cried as I tried to defend myself.

"The hell you didn't. My grand baby told me about how you were always putting your hands on my daughter!" Sadie's mom said.

"Ma'am, Sadie and I had our problems, I'll admit that, but I would never want to kill her. She was pregnant with my seed. I would've never hurt her that way," I said as

I looked into her eyes. I just wanted her to see the sincerity in my eyes and believe me. Maybe if I could get Sadie's mom to believe in my innocence, she could help me with the cops.

"LIAR!" Melinda shouted. It took everything in me not to snap on her ass.

I looked at Sadie with tears in my eyes. I couldn't believe that our baby was gone. My eyes wandered down to her now flattened stomach as tears threatened to fall. Our baby was no longer there.

"Who the fuck would do some shit like this?" I asked as I looked at Sadie.

"That's what we want to know!" a female cop in street clothes wearing her badge on her hip shot at me as she entered the room.

Sadie began stirring around in the bed a bit. Both me and the officer stepped closer to her.

"Come in here, quick!" She immediately got on her radio and had two uniformed pigs rush in like they were about to hem a nigga up and shit.

"Sadie tell them I didn't do this to you! Tell them who did it! They're tryna arrest me baby! Tell them who did this shit!" I demanded with tears streaming from my eyes.

Opening her right eye, while her left was swollen shut, Sadie stared at all of us around her. She looked scared but didn't speak.

"Who did this to you?" the female cop questioned, taking charge.

Looking directly at me, Sadie mumbled, "Joo… Jorrrr… Jordon."

"No, baby! They wanna know who did this shit to you! Tell them!"

"Ma'am, can you tell us who assaulted you?" the short white officer intervened.

"Mommy tell them who hurt you like that! Who did this to you?" Melinda asked.

"Joo… Jorrrr, Jordan…"

"YOU DID THIS?! I KNEW YOU DID IT!" Melinda cried as she started punching me with all her might.

"I DIDN'T DO IT! I DIDN'T DO IT!" I cried.

Beeeeeeeeeeeeeeep…

The machines hooked up to Sadie started going crazy as she closed her eyes and took her last breath.

"MOMMY! MOMMIIIIIEEEEEEE!" Melinda cried as she rushed to her mom's beside. "Mommy, I'm sorry. Don't go mommy! I'll be good from now on!"

Her mom and Melinda were crying like crazy. All I could do was stand there with a blank expression on my face as the cops slapped the cuffs on me and hauled me off.

I felt bad for Sadie, but even worse for myself! *She probably pinned that shit on me on purpose for all the pain I put her through.* Or maybe she wasn't trying to pin it on me at all. Maybe she was trying to tell me she loved me or was sorry she lost the baby. She could've been trying to say anything, but now we'll never know.

My heart and head were fucked up behind the shit, but being the selfish nigga that I was, I couldn't help but think, *There goes my only alibi...*

Chapter Eighteen

Alondra

A few weeks had gone by since the attack. Since then, I had been suffering with a constant headache and cramps. The doctor had prescribed meds, but nothing was helping. It didn't help that I was miserable at home by myself. Lonelier than I had ever felt in my life.

Javion was with his dad and Jordan had finally gotten his ass locked up. I didn't have a friend to save my life. Not even De'vonte. He had been ignoring my calls ever since I sent him all those texts threatening Amerika's job.

"Fuck both of them!" I huffed, slamming my fist on the kitchen counter. "I don't have shit to lose, so fuck it!"

Dialing up Javion's school, I got the principal on the line and drug Amerika's name all through the mud. It felt damn good doing it too. I didn't regret none of that shit until an hour later when my baby daddy called me up flipping out. He talked so bad to me that I was ready to fight his ass, pregnant or not.

"You called the school?" he asked, as if he didn't already know the answer to that question.

"I told you to quit fucking with her or I would. It ain't my fault you didn't believe me. Shit, I gave you fair warning!" I was finally happy that I had won a round.

"You called the school even though I warned you not to?" he asked.

"I warned you that I would! You didn't fuckin' listen to me!"

"Bitch! You don't dictate to me who the fuck I date!" he fumed.

"*Bitch*? DID YOU JUST CALL ME A BITCH?!"

"FUCKIN' RIGHT! That's exactly what the fuck you acting like!"

"I'm the mother of your child!"

"I don't give a fuck! I told you to stop interfering in my fuckin' relationship! Now, you done called up the fuckin' school. You must've thought I was playin' with yo ass when I said I was gon' cut you off, huh? But guess what? Now that you done fucked up by calling the school, I'ma cut yo ass off and take care of Amerika! How bout that?"

"Are you serious right now, De'vonte? You gon' cut me off and take care of her ass? You're supposed to take care of me!" I cried, getting all kinds of angry. Who the hell did he think he was? Why was he being so cruel to me? Didn't he realize that he and my son were all I had left? Of course, I had my baby, but he wasn't here yet. I couldn't believe De'vonte was acting this way toward me behind a smart bitch.

"I'M SUPPOSED TO TAKE CARE OF MY SON! AND MY SON LIVES WITH ME, SO HE WILL GET TAKEN CARE OF! YOU… YOU CAN GO KILL YOURSELF SOMEWHERE!" he said. I almost choked on my tongue hearing that. He really didn't give a fuck about me. "DON'T EVER CALL ME AGAIN!"

"You don't mean that…" I cried as tears ran down my cheeks. "De'vonte! DE'VONTE, ANSWER ME!" There was no response, so I pulled my phone from my ear and the line was dead. I couldn't believe he had hung up in my face. I dialed his number back, but he didn't pick up… not the first, second, third, or fourth time.

"UGH! Just wait until I have this baby! I'm gonna fuck that bitch Amerika up and De'vonte. I might not be able to beat his ass, but he's gonna know he's been in a fuckin' fight!" I yelled out mad that I couldn't have a drink. Lord knew I needed one. "Ugh!" I yelled out as I clinched my stomach.

I had been having Braxton-Hicks lately, but this was much different. This time I felt that shit in my back and legs.

Trying to keep myself busy, I began doing a load of laundry and took a shower. When I stepped out and dried off, I got a sharp stabbing sensation in my stomach then noticed a little blood on the towel. "What the fuck? Am I in labor?"

As the pain began to cease, I began getting dressed. I had a good idea I was about to have my baby.

Sliding into my cheetah print leggings, another pain hit. It doubled me over and had me crying real tears.

Snatching my cell back up, I dialed for emergency services. Instead of staying on the line with me, they just told me to hang tight and they would send an ambulance.

Frustrated out of my mind, I threw my phone up against the wall and began to cry as I paced the floor barefoot. The first sound I heard, I flew to the door and snatched it open.

"Bitch you must be crazy calling up to my fuckin' job like that!" Amerika shouted as I dropped to the floor with blood leaking from between my legs. "Oh, my goodness!"

Amerika tried to help me, like she did before, and I was just as mean. "Get ya fuckin' hands off me!"

"You need to go to the hospital, stupid!" Amerika screamed in a panic as she got down on the floor beside me and tried to comfort me.

"I don't need your fuckin' help! The ambulance is on its way!" I tried to convince her as the biggest pain I ever felt in my life hit me. I hollered out in agony.

"Please! Let me help you Alondra! We don't have time to wait on the fuckin' ambulance!"

Knowing she was right, I let her clinch my arm and help me to my feet. "Oh, shit!" I cried even harder as I saw the big puddle of blood on the floor beneath me. "My baby!"

"Come on!"

Amerika laced her arm under my arm and struggled to get me to the car. Sliding me onto her cream-colored leather seats, I felt the thick liquid smearing under me. I knew that I was making a big ass mess in her nice ride, but I was in too much pain to give a fuck.

"Hang in there Alondra! I'm gonna get you some help!" Amerika jumped behind the wheel and broke every traffic law known to man to get me to the hospital. She even prayed for me along the way.

Where this bitch come from? Is she actually trying to help me?

Finding myself getting wrapped up in my emotions was a great distraction from my pain, until we suddenly got stuck in traffic. Then panic set in.

"I wanna push!" I screamed.

"No! Don't push Alondra!"

Thinking quickly, Amerika threw the car in park, got out and ran around to my side. When she opened my door and reached across me to unbuckle my seatbelt, another contraction hit. I had no control over what came next.

"Oh, shit!" Amerika frowned up as she watched my water bust all in her front passenger seat.

"I'm sorry!" I yelled out and grabbed on to her tightly.

Lifting me up, Amerika's big ass carried me in her arms. I locked my arms around her neck but then became nauseous. "Ugh!"

Vomit came spewing out my mouth all over Amerika's clothes and face. She swiped her face with her shoulder and kept going. I didn't see how because that shit stunk like the liver and onions I had eaten earlier.

"I gotta get you there!" Amerika panted heavily as she stepped off the second curb. My head suddenly began spinning and I felt my body going limp. I must've blacked out because when I woke up, I no longer saw Amerika. I could've sworn I was now in the arms of a strong handsome black man. I remember thinking, "God sent me an angel…"

Before I could reach up and touch his face to make sure he was real, I passed out again…

The next time I came to, I was in a recovery room at the hospital and my stomach wasn't big any more. Yes, a bitch went crazy.

"Where's my baby? Did I lose my baby! Did my baby die?" I yelled as loud as I could.

Several doctors rushed over to me and began restraining me until a nurse came towards me with a filled syringe. She immediately inserted it into my IV and I was knocked out once again.

When I felt myself begin to come out of my induced sleep, I was scared to open my eyes. I just laid still and prayed that it was all one big nightmare.

Slowly moving my right hand from my side to my tummy, I felt the emptiness once again. Tears began to flow before I could force my eyes open.

"Alondra? I'm here! It's me, Amerika!" she whispered, gaining my attention.

Approaching my bed, she smiled and held on to my palm. "You scared me!"

"Where… where's my…"

"Your healthy son is in the nursery. He had some breathing complications, but the handsome lil guy is doing just fine!" she assured me bringing a smile to my face. "The nurse should be coming back with him any minute."

"Thanks," I sighed in relief.

No matter how hard I tried to be mad at Amerika and hate her, I couldn't. I just wasn't ready to be nice to her quite yet.

"Damn, you really tried to carry a bitch too, huh?" I laughed, drawing my hand from hers.

"Yeah, shit, I didn't want you to lose your baby, Alondra!"

"I appreciate you," I thanked her.

"No worries."

"I must've passed out a time or two, huh?" I asked remembering the stranger. "I must've been delirious too shit!"

"Yeah, you blacked out…"

"I swear when you were carrying me, I saw a man. He was dressed like a construction worker and he was so fine, girl!"

"You weren't dreaming Alondra! That was Jerron. He carried you the rest of the way here and wouldn't leave until you woke up!"

"Ah, hi," he stuttered with his gorgeous grin as he approached my bed. "I hope you don't mind. I was just so worried about you. That was a lot of blood you lost!"

My eyes wondered all over Jerron's clothing and noticed that I had made a mess all over him too. I felt bad, but not as good as I felt seeing his handsome ass standing there concerned about lil' ol me.

As I got wrapped up in a full conversation with Jerron, the nurse came in with my son. Instead of handing him to me, she handed him to Jerron. Shit, she probably thought he was the father.

"Congratulations!" she sang out before leaving.

Jerron laughed as he stared down at my baby before handing him to me. "He's a nice-looking healthy boy! Congrats Alondra."

The way my name rolled off Jerron's tongue had my body quivering. He was not only handsome, he was kind, loving and had a good ass legitimate job! I never messed with a guy like that, but I was looking forward to it.

Getting so wrapped up in my new friend, I didn't even notice that Amerika had left. *Oh well...*

Chapter Nineteen

Amerika

The whole ordeal with Alondra had me shook and drained. I had never seen a baby delivered and I had a whole new respect for all mothers. When she woke up, she seemed to be a whole different person. Hell, she was even a little nice. I knew it all had to do with Jerron, the cute construction worker that came to her rescue and mine. Her ass was heavy as fuck!

It was nice of him, but I didn't think he was going to fall for Alondra. I mean, once he sat there with me and watched her give birth to her son right in the hospital lobby, I honestly thought he was gonna jet out. Nah, he stood his ground and waited for her. All the while, he told me a little about himself.

The 32-year old widow lost his pregnant wife and unborn child a year prior when she had complications during delivery from leukemia. Jerron's story was so sad it had me crying like a baby! Then, when he told me about how he donated half the life insurance money to cancer research, I lost it. Good men like him were rare and I prayed that he didn't get mixed up with Alondra if she didn't change her ways.

Not wanting to be in the middle, I silently excused myself and left the hospital. "Wow!"

Not believing what type of day I had, I dialed De'vonte up. He answered like he was expecting my call. "You cool, baby?"

"Yeah, I'm actually good," I sang out happily.

"Damn, you sound good too, for someone who just got fired behind some bullshit!" De'vonte huffed heavily into the phone.

"You said you got me though, right?" I teased, knowing that I had enough money saved to survive for a year if I had to.

"No doubt, baby," he replied. "What shifted your mood?"

"When I left the school, after getting humiliated and gathering all my shit, I took my ass right on over to Alondra's…"

"Oh, shit, Amerika!"

"Yeah, I went over there, and I wanted to beat the shit out of her ass too!"

"You know she's big and pregnant and you too old to be fighting…"

"I'm not old, I beg yo pardon De'vonte!" I teased then explained how Alondra already had the baby.

After I told him everything in detail, he began yelling out like he was disgusted. "She got blood and all that shit in yo ride, baby?"

"Yeah, I'm pulling up at the detail shop right now. While it's getting cleaned, I'm gonna run into this 'Ross Dress for Less' and get something to throw on. They gave me a pair of too small scrubs at the hospital and I'm running around looking a hot ass mess."

"No, don't change baby! Come home so we can play doctor!"

"Boy bye! You have got to see this shit on me. I look like a busted can of Pillsbury biscuits!" I said as we cracked up laughing. That was what I loved about De'vonte. No matter what I went through, he was always so supportive of me. I never imagined he could make me feel that way.

The way I felt about him and the way he treated me had me thinking that I should stop judging people by their looks. As thuggish as my man is, I would've never known how great he actually was had he not changed my tire that day. *Who would've thought having a flat tire would change my life the way that it had?* I was in love with a thuggish, ruggish bone and I wasn't ashamed of that one bit.

"Well, I'm waiting on you whenever you get here," he said.

"Okay, I won't be long."

"I ain't never met nobody like you before Amerika. You have such a good and kind heart. I mean, all the shit that Alondra put you through and you still helped her…" he admonished.

"I'm no saint, De'vonte. I saw a person in need, so I had to help her regardless of what she has done to try and hurt me. She's Javion's mother and I couldn't let her lose that precious little boy," I said.

"That's why I love you."

"I love you too. I'll see you soon."

We ended the call and I went about getting my car detailed. As I looked over at the passenger's seat, which was covered in blood, I wasn't disgusted about it. I was actually proud of myself. I had pushed everything Alondra had done to make my life miserable to the side and at the end of the day, I had saved the life of her and her newborn. I felt really good about what I had done today.

Chapter Twenty

De'vonte

You ever had a moment where you looked back on your life and wished you had done something differently? That was how I was feeling today. Finding out that I had a daughter was a life changing moment. Meeting her for the first time sent chills down my spine. She was so beautiful.

It all happened a couple of weeks ago. Soon as I saw her, all I wanted to do was hold her and take care of her. I had already missed so much of her life. I still held no bitter feelings toward Cheryl for what she did. She had to do what she felt was right at the time. I was just glad she finally told me the truth.

After meeting Amaya, I wanted to run home and share the news with Amerika. I mean, there was no reason to keep the secret anymore now that Cheryl tagged a murder charge onto his rap sheet that the feds were trying to pin on me. Of course, I had done the crime and I hadn't asked her to help me out that way, but she did. I'd always be grateful to her for that and for giving me a daughter. Now I just had to come clean about everything to Amerika.

After speaking to her about how she played Captain Save a Ho' with Alondra, I was even more proud to have her as my woman. She always went above and beyond for someone.

Who would have ever thought that I would be in love with a smart chick like that? I had run through so many hood chicks in my time because that was where I was from.

They said to never forget where you came from, so I was giving back to the community in a way. Amerika was so different than a hood chick. Most hood chicks were on government assistance, including Section 8 and food stamps. Not Amerika.

She had a career with big time goals to help children, troubled kids at that. She worked hard at what she did, and it would soon pay off when she stepped into her own school for the first time. The proposal had went through and the ground work had begun. Alondra thought she had caused so much scandal that Amerika would leave me and lose her career forever. *Shit, not on my watch.*

Amerika didn't need that job at the school when she could be running her own school. I had so many plans for that woman.

Ring, Buzz, Ring, Buzz...

I was sitting in the living room playing MotoGP 18 on my PlayStation 4 when my phone began to ring. I didn't recognize the number, so I let it go to voicemail. A couple of seconds later, it started to ring again. I looked at the screen and it was the same fuckin' number. Whoever it was must have either had the wrong number or really needed to speak to a nigga.

"Hello?"

"Hello, I need to speak with De'vonte Alexander," said the woman's voice on the other line.

Shit, I didn't know whether to say it was me or lie, so I just told the truth. "This is he."

"De'vonte, you don't know me, but I'm Cheryl's mother…" My body immediately became rigid as I turned the television off and jumped out of my seat. For her to be calling me, this couldn't be a social call. I could hear the woman sniffling in the background. *This can't be good.*

"Is Cheryl alright?" Was the first question that came out of my mouth. Then I had to know if my little girl was okay. "Is Amaya okay?"

"Amaya is fine and the reason why I am calling you. My daughter was killed today…" I almost dropped the phone and fell to the floor. Her words hit me like a ton of bricks. I had just spoken to Cheryl yesterday. How could she be gone now?

"What?" I asked, my voice barely above a whisper from the shock of the news.

"My daughter, Cheryl was killed today," the woman repeated as she continued to sob and sniffle on the other end of the line.

"How did this happen? I just spoke to her yesterday."

"I had just spoken to her a couple of hours ago, so imagine my surprise…" She stopped talking as she broke down on the phone.

"Ma'am, is someone with you? Where are you?" I asked.

"I'm down at the morgue."

"I'm on my way!" I said and quickly hung the phone up. I didn't know if she was by herself or not, but this was definitely a conversation to be had in person.

Grabbing my keys, I rushed out the door then hopped in my ride and headed down to the morgue.

*****

About half an hour later, I pulled into the parking lot and rushed inside. Right away, I found an older version of Cheryl sitting on a bench. The woman was surrounded by a couple of family members, I assumed. When she saw me, they stood up and walked over to me. I didn't know the lady, but I put my arms around her anyway once she gestured me in for a hug. I couldn't even imagine the pain that she was feeling right now.

"I am so sorry for your loss," I said as she cried against my chest. She pushed herself out of my arms after a few minutes. "Cheryl was a wonderful woman and a great federal agent."

The woman nodded her head and said, "Thank you."

"Do they know who did it?" I asked.

"They have the dude in custody. My cousin was trying to serve him with a warrant and he opened fire on her and the other agents." A young man with them answered.

I had heard about shit like that happening, but never knew anyone who had been through it. "Say what?! I thought they wore bullet proof vests when they had to do that," I replied confused.

"She was. The creep shot her in the head. The coroner said she died instantly, so she didn't know what hit her," the young man explained.

"De'vonte, my daughter left this for you," Cheryl's mom said as she handed me an envelope. "She told me that she finally told you about Amaya and she was so happy about it. She had taken care of all this paperwork and told me that if anything ever happened to her, I was to give you this and make sure that Amaya went to live with you."

"What?" I asked as my mouth dropped open. "Amaya is coming to live with me?"

"She's your daughter, but I can certainly take her home to live with me if you don't want her…"

"Oh no ma'am! That's not what I'm saying at all and please forgive me if I gave you that impression. I'm just in shock, ya know?"

"We're all in shock, but this is what my daughter wanted. I have no problem sending my grand baby off to live with you, but you have to promise me that you won't ever exclude me from her life. I'm the only grandparent she's had since my husband died last year. Now, my daughter's dead and I won't lose my grand baby," the woman said.

"I promise that I'll never keep you from Amaya," I said, and I meant it. This woman had been through enough already. I wouldn't be able to live with myself if I didn't allow her to see Amaya.

"Good, you can come by the house and get some of her things. She's at the Lucky Charms Daycare, so you can pick her up from there. I'd do it, but I have to plan my daughter's funeral," she said as she started to cry again.

"Okay, thank you so much… I'm sorry, but I didn't get your name," I said.

"It's Virginia, but everyone calls me Ginny," she said.

"Okay Ginny."

We walked out of the building and to our vehicles. I sat in my truck thinking about Cheryl and how I was going to have to tell Amaya that she was going to be living with me from now on. I didn't know how to tell a three-year-old that her mother was gone. Then it hit me… I needed to tell Javion and Amerika about Amaya first.

My phone began to ring, and it was Amerika. I dried my eyes and picked up.

"Hey baby," I said, trying to sound normal.

"Hey, I thought you said you were going to be home when I got here. Where are you?" she asked.

"I had something to do real quick, but I'll be home soon."

"What's the matter?"

"What do you mean?" I asked.

"There's something off in your voice. What happened?" Amerika pressed.

"I'll explain everything when I get home. I shouldn't be too long."

"Okay. I'm gonna go start dinner then."

"That's great, baby. I'll see you soon."

I ended the call before she had a chance to respond. I didn't mean to, but my world had been turned upside down. Cheryl was gone and now, I had to break the news to our daughter.

"Lord, if you're listening, please give me some guidance. I don't know how I'm going to do this," I said.

Remembering the envelope that Ginny gave me, I quickly tore it open.

De'vonte, if you are reading this letter, it means that I got tied up in my work and am no longer here. I'm sorry for not telling you sooner about Amaya. I never meant to keep her from you, but I just couldn't risk anything happening to her. I want you to take Amaya into your home and raise her. Be the father to her that I know you can be. You two have missed out on a lot already, so don't let my death keep you from each other anymore. She's your daughter. I know the transition will be a little rough at first, but eventually, you both will learn to live without me.

Please take care of our daughter and don't ever let her forget me. Tell her that mommy loved her more than anything in this world and that one day, we'll be together again. Also, please allow my family to spend some time with her from time to time. They're the only family she's known throughout her life, so I don't want them taken from her. I filed for a new birth certificate and added your name as the father. It's in a box on my dresser, along with a safe deposit key giving you permission to remove the contents for Amaya.

Please take care of my baby and let her know I'll always love her. Thank you for stepping up. Know that I'll always have a special place in my heart for you. Yours truly, Cheryl

By the time I finished reading that letter, I was crying like a pussy. I dried my eyes and started my truck. I had a little girl to pick up and introduce to her brother and stepmom to be. Yep, I was going to marry Amerika one day, probably real soon.

Arriving at the daycare, I pulled myself together and became the man I had to be. Yes, I was already a father, but this was a whole new ball game. I never had to explain death to anyone. I mean, how could I when I didn't understand the shit myself?

"Hello, I'm Amaya's father, De'vonte Alexander."

"I'm so sorry for your loss. Cheryl and I are… were really close. I've been watching Amaya since she was six months old. I can't believe that she's gone," the girl at the desk stated with tears in her eyes. "You can go back and get Amaya. I need to get myself together."

Looking away from her so I wouldn't get to crying again, I went behind the glass enclosure to find Amaya. Even though there were dozens and dozens of kids, it wasn't hard to spot my daughter. She always wore those old school bright colored yarned ribbons. That day she had on lime green ones to match her multicolored romper she wore.

"Daddy!" she shrieked happily like she had been around me her whole life.

As she jumped in my arms, she squeezed me tightly and told me I smelled good. Burying her nose into my neck, she giggled playfully.

"Where's mommy?"

My heart sank as my smile disappeared. I wasn't ready to face her, but I sucked it up and placed her on her little feet. "She's gone away for a while. How about you stay with me until it's time to see her again."

The tears tried to force their way out, but I held on to every last one and took a deep breath as I stared into Amaya's big brown doe eyes.

"Okay daddy, but I'm hungry. Can we go to Red Lobster?"

"What?" I laughed as I grabbed her backpack and held her hand all the way to my truck. "You don't wanna get a Happy Meal from McDonald's with the little toy in it?"

"Daddy, mommy said no fast food!" she sang out with a serious look, then busted out giggling when I strapped her into the built-in car seat that I never in a million years thought I would be using. I deemed the feature useless until today.

"Wow! This truck is amazing!" Amaya yelled out as she started running her small palms over everything within her reach. I hurried up and clicked the child safety lock on her door before closing it, then locked the windows before pulling off. All the parenting skills I possessed were quickly coming back to me.

Okay, this might not be as bad as I thought it would be. That thought sounded good, but panic set in when she screamed out like she was in pain.

"Daddy, I gotta go potty!"

"Okay, when we get to Red Lobster, you can go pee."

"No, I gotta poop!"

Oh, hell nah! I ranted silently, not knowing what to do but call Amerika and have her meet me there. I knew she was cooking, but she was going to have to put it up because this was an emergency!

Chapter Twenty-One

Amerika

When De'vonte called me yelling about meeting him at Red Lobster, knowing good and well I cooked, I thought there was something seriously wrong. I wasn't about that street life, but I was definitely taking my pepper spray with me.

Snatching my keys, I shot out the house and drove ten minutes to the restaurant to see what the fuss was about. "I see his car. Where is he?"

Assuming he was already inside, I entered and asked the hostess working if there was an Alexander party seated already. She checked the list and shook her head no. "I don't see any Alexander on here. Maybe, he's here. If you wanna go around and look."

"Thanks," I spoke nonchalantly while dialing De'vonte. He answered out of breath.

"Where are you?"

"I'm here! Where are you?" I replied still looking around.

"I'm in the restroom..."

"Okay, well I'm here..."

"No, I need you to come in here!"

"What?!" I whispered loudly like he was out of his damn mind. "I'm not going in the men's restroom De'vonte! What's wrong with you?"

"Please, I need you!" he said in desperation.

Going against my better judgement, I eased by the short blonde waitress and scooted in the men's room. "De'vonte?" I called out.

The door to the restroom stall opened and there he was, standing there nearly in tears as he pointed to the toilet. Moving closer, I saw the two little feet swinging. "Who's that?"

"This is Amaya and I really didn't want you to meet her like this, but…"

"Huh?"

"I'm done!" the beautiful little girl sang out holding up the balled-up toilet paper. "I need help wiping, daddy!"

Daddy? Did that little girl just refer to my man as her daddy? What the hell was really going on here? De'vonte had better have a darn good explanation for this shit.

"Daddy?" I repeated looking from Amaya to De'vonte noticing the resemblance right away.

"Yes, and if you help me, I can tell you all about it."

Rushing to assist the small child, I took her hand and made her wipe herself in order to teach her. She said thank you, flushed and ran to the sink to wash her hands. I joined her without taking my eyes off De'vonte.

Whispering in my ear, he asked me not to be mad. "Her mom got killed today and she doesn't know what's going on. Can you please help me?"

Now I was feeling bad for getting mad about it. I had a million questions and couldn't ask one. Amaya was right there in earshot talking about shrimp.

"You had me scared calling me like that!" I nudged him playfully as we got seated.

"Shit, you don't think that was an emergency?" he teased and laughed as he opened the pack of four crayons the waiter had brought to the table.

"It was!" I agreed with a smile watching Amaya write her name on the paper. "How old is she?"

"Three..."

"And she's writing her own name?" I gasped impressed beyond belief.

"Yes, and I can speak Spanish too!" Amaya sang proudly as she began counting. "Uno, dos, tres..."

As this bright beautiful little girl not only counted to twenty in Spanish, she recited the colors and alphabet as well. She had all the patrons in the restaurant cheering her on.

"No way she's three!" I shouted again before we ordered our food.

As Amaya specifically chanted off what she wanted to eat, I leaned over to De'vonte. "So, is she going with relatives?"

"Yeah, she's staying with her father," he grinned, raising both his brows.

"I think that's great!" I said, becoming a little nervous about his lifestyle. "You know what that means, right?"

"Ain't even worried about it baby. You're opening that school right on time. I'm investing in the transportation and the afterschool programs. That itself is gonna generate a steady income. Money ain't an issue because you know my savings is straight. Don't worry about nothing."

"So, am I a part of this… this… this family plan?"

"I sure hope so. I want you to be." De'vonte said as he leaned across and pecked my lips.

"Oooooo," Amaya giggled, pointing at both of us.

"Hush girl and color daddy a picture." De'vonte teased and tickled his daughter making her laugh even harder.

The two of them were so cute together. It was so sad that her mother was killed. De'vonte never mentioned her that I could remember. I couldn't wait to hear the story behind that one!

The animated late lunch lasted over an hour, then we headed to De'vonte's in two separate cars. The entire ride, I wondered how it would be to have his child. He was so good with kids and I loved them. I found myself fantasizing until I got back to the house a few minutes after them.

"Where's Amaya?" I questioned when I saw him changing his clothes into his gym shorts and T-shirt.

"She fell asleep in the car. I almost forgot it was Friday!" De'vonte panted as he slipped into his new red and white Jordans. "Javion has practice at the Boys and Girls Club."

"Oh, yeah, Mr. Sexy Coach!" I wooed as I went in for a kiss.

"You got jokes baby," he laughed kissing me back. "Can you watch Amaya for me? I wanna have some time after practice alone with Javion. I need to explain about his little sister."

Shit, I didn't know the story my own damn self, but I agreed. I was actually looking forward to it.

"Okay, when she gets up, I wanna take her shopping. Is that okay?" I asked, getting amped to buy the beautiful princess whatever her heart desired. I couldn't help but want to spoil her after losing her mother.

"Yes, would you please?" he smiled, taking his wallet from the dresser and drew a black platinum card out. "Cheryl's mother said she would send her things, but she doesn't have anything for now. She's in the guest room next to mine. I wanna fix it up a little with some girly things."

"Keep your card babe," I told him. "Let me do this for her. It will be our bonding time. I can get to know her a little better."

De'vonte neared me and took me into an embrace. With his eyes watering, he bent down to press his cool soft lips against mine. "You gotta be heaven sent baby. No woman I know would be so loving and understanding. I love you."

"I love you too," I whispered before giggling to break up the emotional moment. "You better get outta here before you're late. I already cooked, so dinner will be warm by the time you two get back."

Just barking out family plans made me feel more like a woman than I had ever felt. I never dreamed it would be so overwhelmingly wonderful.

You'd think I'd be salty about losing my job and my reputation smeared, but I wasn't. I was looking forward to the next phase of my life.

"Okay, what now?" I sighed as I idled in the kitchen.

As bad as I wanted a glass of wine, I bypassed it and poured some orange juice. After sipping a bit, I went in and checked on Amaya.

"Oh, she's so beautiful," I whispered as I eased into the room and tiptoed to the bedside.

"Thank you," she mumbled, sitting up in the bed. "My mommy's still gone?"

Closing my eyes and taking in a breath of air, I held my tears and smiled before looking down at Amaya's innocent little face. "Yes, she is honey, but we're gonna keep you busy, okay?"

"Busy?" she giggled, bundling herself up in the fluffy white down comforter.

"You wanna go shopping?" I asked watching her eyes widen.

"Can we go to the Disney store?!" she yelled jumping up into my arms. The strawberry scent from her hair invaded my nostrils as she embraced me tightly.

"Sure!" I answered, rubbing my hands in her locks. "Can I put your hair in two braids first?"

"Yes! I like when mommy does my hair like that!" she shrieked then held her hands between her legs. "I gotta go potty!"

"Okay, let me take you," I offered.

"I just gotta pee-pee, so you don't have to come," she said like a big girl as she grinned showing her deep dimples.

Showing her to the adjoining guest bathroom, I left the door partially open just in case she needed me. "I'm done!" Amaya yelled out before the toilet flushed. "I can't reach the water to wash my hands!"

"We'll get you a stepstool while we're out shopping," I told her while turning the faucet on before holding her light body in the air.

"You are so sweet, Miss Amerika!"

"You don't have to call me that," I laughed. "You can just call me Amerika."

"I like Miss Amerika! You're like a queen and I'm like a princess," she teased looking at her reflection in the mirror. "Mommy is a queen too. You are pretty just like her!"

"Awwww, thank you!" I hummed ready to cry again. I didn't know what it was, but I was ready to bust out in tears about every little thing. It was becoming uncontrollable.

Hurrying to comb her hair and giving her a light snack, Amaya and I headed out to the mall. I was just as thrilled about going as she was…

Chapter Twenty-Two

De'vonte

"Daddy, when is mommy coming back to get me? Doesn't she miss me?" Amaya asked.

I looked at Amerika because I wasn't prepared to have this conversation with my daughter. But I guess now was as good a time as any since the funeral was scheduled for tomorrow.

"Come here baby and sit next to daddy and Amerika," I said as I patted my lap.

She ran and jumped on my lap. I took a deep breath and she asked, "What's wrong daddy?"

"I need to talk to you about your mommy."

"What about her? Is she coming today? I miss her so much," Amaya said with a huge smile on her face.

"No baby, she's not coming today."

"Why not? Doesn't she love me anymore?" Amaya asked with the sad puppy dog eyes.

I looked over at Amerika because I was unsure what to say. "Your mommy loves you very much, honey. That's not why she isn't here," Amerika said with tears in her eyes.

"Baby, your mommy had an accident at work..."

"Oh my God! Is she okay? Is mommy okay?" Amaya asked.

"No baby. See, mommy went to sleep…" I had to pause because that shit didn't sound right to me. I didn't know how to explain that shit to her. How do you tell a three-year old that her mom was gone forever? "You know how there are angels in heaven?"

"Yes, with pretty white gowns and halos and wings!" she explained. As smart as she was, I just knew that she would know what angels were.

"Well, God called mommy to his home to be one of those angels…"

"What?" Amaya asked.

"Your mommy is a beautiful angel now with a halo and wings," I said as tears filled my eyes. I hoped that she understood what I was saying without me having to say the actual words.

"My mommy is an angel?" she asked.

I heard sniffling and looked over at Amerika as she dried her eyes. "Yes baby. Do you understand what your daddy is trying to tell you?" Amerika asked.

"If mommy is an angel, why didn't she take me with her? I wanna be an angel with her too!" Amaya said.

"In time, we'll all be angels. God handpicks his special angels every day, but he wanted you to stay with me, Amerika, and Javion. Do you understand?" I asked.

"I think so," she said as her lips trembled and tears flowed from her pretty little eyes. "Mommy's in heaven." She leaned against me and cried harder than I had ever wanted to hear her cry. Me and Amerika wrapped our arms around her and each other until she was okay.

Amerika went to give her a bath a few minutes later and we both tucked her into bed. Once Amaya was sound asleep, we tiptoed out of the room and went to the bedroom. Amerika wrapped her arms around me in a tight embrace.

"What's that for?" I asked.

"Because I thought you could use it. You handled that talk with Amaya wonderfully," she said.

"Thanks, babe. I couldn't have done it without you. I'm wondering if I should take her to the funeral tomorrow. I mean, she's so young. I don't know if her viewing her mother's body is a good idea. It might do more harm than good."

"I know it's going to be hard, but I think she should be there. I think she should be able to say goodbye to her mom one last time."

"I don't know, Amerika. I think it might be too much for her," I said.

"Whatever you decide, I'll support you a hundred percent. I just think that since she never really got to say goodbye to her mom, she should be able to do that tomorrow. It might help her understand that Cheryl isn't coming back," Amerika said. "Just sleep on it and decide in the morning."

"Okay." We took a shower and got in bed. Since I had so much on my mind, all I did was hold her that night. My dick was too depressed to get up and do the job.

*****

The next morning, I woke up feeling a bit apprehensive about today's events. I had decided that Amerika was right, and I was going to bring Amaya to the funeral. I thought it would be a great idea for her to see her mom that last time and be comforted by people she knew and was familiar with. Even though I was her father, I came into her life pretty late. I was still getting to know my daughter.

Amerika and I slid out of bed and took care of our morning rituals. "Have you made a decision, babe?" she asked as I brushed my teeth.

"Yea," I said as I spit out the toothpaste. "I decided that you were right. Amaya will need today for closure." I gurgled the mouthwash, spit it out and cleaned up my face.

"You're making the right decision," she said with a smile. "I'm going to go get dressed and get Amaya up.

"Thanks babe."

"No thanks needed," she said as she stood on her tiptoes to give me a kiss. She walked out of the room and I followed behind her a short time later.

Once we were dressed, we headed to the funeral home. Upon arrival, the first thing we noticed were the abundance of police motorcycles and cars parked everywhere. I hoped that I'd be able to find a parking spot.

"Woooow!" Amaya exclaimed as she looked at all the vehicles. "That's a lot of police!"

"Yep, they're here because they loved your mommy," Amerika said.

We finally found a parking spot and headed inside. I wished I had known so many people would be here, I would've stayed my ass at home. I hated the fuckin' po po's, so I certainly didn't want to be around them at all. Shit, my skin itched as I walked by them mu'fuggas.

As we made our way to the front of the funeral home, Amaya took a deep breath and started screaming for her mommy to wake up. That was the reason I didn't want to bring her. All eyes were on us as I tried to keep her from jumping down to get to her mom.

"MOMMYYYYYYY!" she cried in my arms as I tried to hold her back. "MOMMYYYYY WAKE UP!"

"Amaya calm down baby!" I soothed. "Mommy's sleeping. Remember when I told you she had her wings last night!"

"I WANT MY MOMMY!" she screamed.

Her grandmother stood up and with tears in her eyes, she tried to comfort Amaya. Amaya wasn't having it. She was kicking and screaming for her mom, so we had no choice but to leave the services. As I carried her out, she continued to holler for her mommy. There wasn't a dry eye in that place as we walked out the door. My heart was breaking for this sweet little girl. I didn't know what to do to help her.

As I unlocked the truck, Amerika and I both got in the back seat with Amaya. She was still crying for her mom. "Amaya please, baby listen to us," Amerika soothed.

"I- want- mommy!" she sobbed.

"Baby, I'm so sorry but mommy went to heaven. We talked about this last night," I tried to explain.

"I- want- mommy," she repeated as Amerika wiped the tears and snot from her face. We both had tears in our eyes as we tried to get Amaya settled in her seat.

"I know baby, but your mommy will always be with you. She'll always be right here," Amerika said as she touched her finger to Amaya's chest where her heart beat was. "Whenever you want your mommy, all you have to do is close your eyes and she'll be with you."

Amaya closed her eyes and that seemed to calm her down enough to strap her in the seat. Amerika clicked the seatbelt in and I slipped out and got behind the wheel to drive us home.

All I could do was pray for God to help us get through this horrible time for my daughter's sake.

Chapter Twenty-Three

Alondra

The day came for me to leave the hospital, and I honestly didn't have anyone to call to pick me up. While I sat on the edge of the bed debating whether or not to pull up my Uber app, Javion called me screaming and hollering about having a sister! He almost gave me a heart attack!

"What the hell are you talking about Javion?! I had a little boy! You have a brother!"

"No, I know that mom! I'm talking about Amaya. Her mother is Cheryl…"

That name stabbed me deep enough to begin to shake. That was the bitch that interfered in me and De'vonte's relationship. I hated that bitch with a fucking passion, especially because she was a cop! I knew that he was using her to help him out of some trouble about four or five years prior, but I never knew he was fucking her!

"Javion please calm down, son. I just had a baby and excitement ain't that good for me right now. Are you sure about this?" I asked feeling sick to my stomach. I was supposed to be the only one to have De'vonte's child! I was the special one! Shit, at least that was what I thought.

"Mom, Amaya is staying with us…"

"Wait… what?!" I yelled out becoming upset.

"Yes, mom!"

Not wanting to involve Javion in me and his father's affairs, I bit my tongue and told him to have

De'vonte call me. I wanted to know what the hell was going on.

"When can I come see my brother, mom?" Javion asked anxiously. "What did you name him?"

"His name is Jaylen." I told him. "I'm going home today, so you can come anytime. I miss you."

"I miss you too mom!" Javion sang out before asking if he could bring his sister too. Of course, he sure could. I had some questions for his father.

After hanging up with my son, I tended to my baby boy who was in need of a diaper change. I quickly took care of it then picked my cell back up to get a ride. Before I could dial out, I got a surprise visitor.

"Hey beautiful!" Jerron sang out, holding a gift bag, balloons and the most amazing floral arrangement. He wasn't in his work clothes. He had on some nice jeans, a tan colored button down and some peanut butter Timbs. That nigga knew he had swag.

"Sorry for just popping back up here, but I haven't been able to stop thinking about you and your son."

He called me beautiful and got me gifts! My heart fluttered, and I was sitting there stuck on stupid not able to push one single word out of my mouth.

"Did I overstep my boundaries?" Jerron asked hesitantly backing up from my bed.

"Oh, no!" I managed to blurt out. "I'm just surprised to see you."

"I hope that's a good thing," he stated boldly with that knockout smile.

"It could be, if you would be willing to give me and my baby a ride home, no strings attached," I added with a flirtatious grin and my coochie wasn't even healed yet.

"What? Yes, I can give you a ride! Are you ready to go now?" he asked.

"Yes, the doctor signed my discharge papers a few minutes ago, so your timing is perfect! I just need to buzz the nurse, so they can wheel me out. You know, I got that V.I.P. service over here."

"As you should."

That man had my heart fluttering like a damn school girl with a crush on the teacher. If I wouldn't have just had a baby and wasn't still bleeding, I was sure my kitty would be leaking a different kind of moisture. She definitely was throbbing behind that ol' bulky maxi pad. I pressed the button and when the nurse asked if I needed anything, I told her I was ready to go.

On any other occasion, she would've asked that question, I would've gotten totally slick at the mouth with her ass. Shit, she knew I was discharged. She knew I had to get the fuck up outta there. Yet, she still asked if I needed something. That was a question screaming for a smart retort, but with Jerron standing there looking all scrumptious and shit, I didn't dare show the hood girl in me... not today at least. I needed to at least reel him in first before he ever saw the LOCA side of me.

The nurse came in a couple of minutes later with the wheelchair and I sat down in it slowly. Jerron carried all the goodies he bought, and the stuff Amerika had sent over and followed us out. I held my precious little boy against me thinking how sad it was going to be for me to have to raise another little black boy as a single mother. This world was fucked up enough and I wanted to give my son a better life in a two-parent household, but just because Jordan was the dad didn't mean our household would've been better than any other family.

Jordan was a tyrant and his antics had finally gotten him caught all the way up. I couldn't believe that he killed Sadie. I couldn't stand the little ghetto groupie, but I never would've wished her dead. However, now that she was, and Jordan was out of my life, the world was already a better place. *Rest in hell bitches!*

I just knew after everything Sadie had put me through that the devil was roasting her ass like chestnuts on an open fire at Christmas. I wondered what her last thoughts were about. I wondered if she had any regrets about anything that she did.

"I'm gonna go get my truck," Jerron said placing my attention on him again as the elevator came to the first floor. I hadn't noticed that I had been spaced out that whole ride down. Not anymore though. As I watched Jerron's sexy ass walk out the door, all I could do was smile.

"You and your husband must be very happy," the nurse said, referring to Jerron.

"Oh, yes we are honey... yes we are!" I said with a smile. That man was so damn fine, he could make me forget all about my baby daddy. De'vonte and Jordan who?

As I was wheeled out of the double glass doors, Jerron pulled up in a GMC Denali truck. I admired the sleek grey paint job and the chrome rims. Yea, he definitely was a keeper. He had a legit paying job, a fine ass truck, and probably a nice crib too. He would definitely work as a step dad. As he helped me into the back of the truck, I placed Jaylen in the carrier. Jerron strapped it in and closed the door.

Making his way into the driver's seat, he smiled at me before taking off. I was smiling too.

"Take a left when you leave the parking lot," I instructed preparing to guide him to my place. As I got comfortable in the back seat alongside of my new baby boy, I leaned my head against the headrest.

"So, do you have anyone coming to help you with the baby?" he asked.

"I'm not sure. My son will be dropping by to see me later though."

"Your son?" he asked with a raised eyebrow.

"Yes, I have a 14-year old son, but he stays with his daddy."

"14? You don't look old enough to have a teenager."

That caused me to blush so hard, I felt the redness in my panties. "Thanks for the compliment."

"You're welcome. You're a very beautiful woman, Alondra. May I ask where the baby's father is? I don't want to be too nosy, but I'm curious and I'm definitely not trying to intrude or overstep."

"He's locked up doing a big bid. I don't think he's going to be a factor in my baby's life," I admitted. There was no reason to lie to him about where Jordan was or if he was coming back. That nigga was buried so far under the jail, he had his own zip code.

"Oohh, sorry to hear that," Jerron apologized with sincerity.

"Don't be, I'm not. He's right where he needs to be and I'm glad that he's not in my life anymore."

"So, are you single?"

"Very," I chanted sexily. Jerron stayed quiet, but as I side eyed him, I caught him grinning.

"Turn down this street." I pointed to Honeysuckle Lane on the right. He did as I instructed. "Take a left on Rodeo, my house is the fourth one on the left."

My street was called Rodeo Circle, but it should've been called Circus Drive with all the drama that happened there. As we got in eyesight of my home, I gasped in excitement when I saw the stork with the blue balloons tied to it. I knew that Amerika had to be the sappy bitch that set that up, but I was happy. Having her in my corner since the day I gave birth really made me regret getting her fired from her job. I was definitely sorry about that and wished I could take it back.

But, c'est la vie! She'd get over it.

Jerron parked the truck and made his way to the rear passenger's side door to help me out. I grabbed his hand and eased out of the truck.

"Thank you so much," I said. The jolt of electricity that flew through my arm matched the tingling sensation I felt the day I gave birth. Shit, he was in construction, but as many bolts of fire he had flowing through his body, he needed to be an electrician. As the juices flowed through my body all I could think of was how he could set it off.

Grabbing the baby seat, Jerron walked with me to the front door. "May I have your key?" he asked.

I was totally mesmerized by this man. I reached in my bag and handed the keys to him. He unlocked the door and placed the carrier with my sleeping newborn on the sofa then set my keys on the table. "I'll bring the other stuff in."

"Okay," was all I managed to say. *Who is this Superman and where the fuck has he been all my life?* Before he walked out the door, I found my voice. "Jerron?"

"Yea?"

"I'm very single," I said with a smile.

"Good," he said with a smile of his own. "So am I." He walked out the door leaving me standing there needing CPR.

"The Lord is my shepherd and he know what I want!" I said as I looked up at the ceiling. "Lord, you gon' have to stop playin' witcha girl like this!"

I sat down on the sofa next to my baby and tried to keep my breathing steady. I had to be ready to make my next move…

Chapter Twenty-Four

Jordan

I had spent the last two months in fuckin' jail and I was miserable. Jail wasn't for me, even though this wasn't my first rodeo. I had been locked up before, but nothing like this. This time was different than any of those other times because my freedom was being threatened forever. If I got found guilty for killing Sadie, I was never getting out of this muthafucka.

Now I was sitting there anxiously, waiting to meet with my lawyer again about my defense. *As much money as he's costing me, that son of a bitch better have some good news.*

"Mr. Michaels, sorry to keep you waiting," Mr. Martin said when he walked in.

"I ain't been waiting that long. But if you got some good news for me, it don't even matter how long I been waiting," I said in a hopeful tone.

Sitting down across from me, he started pulling stuff out of his briefcase. "Well, I do have some pretty good news for you."

"Is that right? You done found a way to get me up outta here?"

"Not exactly," he said as he opened up his file.

"Not exactly? What the fuck you mean not exactly? I'm paying you some good money to get me the fuck off! Not exactly is NOT AN OPTION!" I yelled. Realizing where I was, I quickly brought my tone back down to normal. "Look, Mr. Martin I didn't do this shit. I loved Sadie and she was carrying my kid. Why would I want to kill her?"

"I don't know the answer to that question, Mr. Michaels. But here's what they're willing to offer you. They'll take the death penalty off the table if you plead guilty to manslaughter."

"I told you that I ain't taking no plea for something I didn't do! I know that shit is the norm for y'all… to get some nigga to plead guilty to lock them up even though they're innocent. Doesn't my innocence matter?" I asked.

I was tired of this bullshit song and dance that I kept having to do with the fuckin' district attorney. They were so anxious to lock my black ass up that they wouldn't even consider that somebody else might have killed that lil bitch. Hell, I knew damn well I wasn't the only nigga she was fuckin'.

"Mr. Michaels, they have a mountain of evidence against you, including the victim's last words before she died pointing the finger at you."

"She wasn't pointing the finger at me! She wanted to tell me that she loved me! Sadie would never do nothing to lock me up! We loved each other!"

"Well, the evidence says otherwise. Not only do they have her dying words, but her neighbors hearing the two of you in an argument before she was killed. Mr. Michaels, I'm doing the best I can here, but you are going to have to face the facts. This evidence against you is strong enough to get a murder conviction. If you don't take this plea deal, you could be sentencing yourself to death."

"Why are they even putting the death penalty on the table? I ain't never been charged with no murder before!"

"You have a whole list of offenses from drug possession to intent to distribute to resisting arrest. The district attorney wants you off the streets and with the election around the corner…"

"They gonna use me as their example, huh?" I said. How the fuck could this have happened?

"I'm afraid so."

"I had an alibi, ya know?"

"Yes, Jackie Cortez. I've been to her house to talk to her. I asked if she's holding back to please come forward. She said she wasn't with you that night. That she was over at some friend's house and he vouched for her," Mr. Martin said.

"Who vouched for her?" I asked.

"Her witness."

"What's his name?"

"Oh, De'vonte Alexander."

When I heard that name, all I could do was laugh hysterically. That nigga had finally beat me. He had finally found a way to lock my ass up for good. For all I knew, he could've killed Sadie's ass, but why? It didn't even make any sense for me to say something to my lawyer because I had no way to prove anything I was saying.

I was going down for a crime I never committed, all because a nigga loved to fuck. "How many years I gotta do?" I asked Mr. Martin's bitch ass. For everything he ain't never did for me, I should've gotten a public defender.

"Twelve and a half to 25," he said.

"TWELVE AND A HALF YEARS?! FOR SOMETHING I DIDN'T DO?!" I screamed. How the fuck could that shit be happening. Mr. Martin jumped back like he thought I was gonna hit him. How the fuck was I gon' do that with these handcuffs on? Stupid muthafucka!

"I'm sorry, Mr. Michaels, but that's the best I can do. They aren't willing to give you less than that because of your history," he said.

"This just ain't fair, man! I know you probably hear a lot of niggas tell you that they're innocent, but I'm a nigga that's telling the truth. I'm really innocent but getting hemmed up on these fuckin' bogus ass charges! I'll be the first to admit that me and Sadie had a rocky relationship, but at the time of her death, I was blowing Jackie's insides out. I don't know why that bitch ain't covering my alibi, but that's some foul shit!" I said in frustration.

"I feel for you, Mr. Michaels, I really do. But the prosecutor isn't going to offer this deal for long. Are you going to take it or go to trial? The choice is yours," the lawyer said.

All that muthafucka was worried about was whether I'd take the deal or not, so he could run back to the DA and let them know he had another black ass for 'em to lock up. I felt like I was losing this battle. By the time I'd be released to see my son by Alondra, he'd be in middle school, if not grown already. This was some bullshit, but what choice did I have. I would just take the deal and battle my case inside. During that time, I was going to get the evidence I needed to put that shit right back on De'vonte, if it took me the whole bid to do it.

"I'll take the fuckin' deal, but make sure you tell those muthafuckas that they locking up an innocent man."

"I'll be sure to let them know, Mr. Michaels. I just need your signature on a couple of documents and the deal will be done. You'll have to go to court and allocate for your crimes before the judge and then you'll be sentenced," he advised.

"What you mean allocate for my crimes?"

"I mean, you'll have to tell the judge what you did."

"I told you I didn't do shit!" I barked refusing to take a fall for another nigga. If I did that, there would be no way to get back at him.

"Right, but the only way the deal will be good is for you to say you did," the lawyer said.

"Nigga, I don't know shit about the crime, so how can I say what happened?"

"What do you mean?"

"I mean, I don't know how she was killed. How many times I gotta say I DIDN'T DO IT?!" I asked.

"Oh, well, that's the only way the deal will stand."

"So, are you gon tell me what to say?" I asked.

"I can't do that. That's against the law."

"Well, I don't know what you want me to do because I didn't do it!" I said through clenched teeth.

I didn't know what was going to happen now, but I hoped they'd let me out of this joint.

Only time would tell…

Chapter Twenty-Five

De'vonte

The last couple of months with Amaya and Javion were incredible. I couldn't believe how much I enjoyed being a father, especially when I taught my kids something new. Each time I did, their faces would light up. That shit was priceless.

While me and my kids were all good on bonding, Amerika had been right there with us. The only thing was, she wasn't there full time and Javion and Amaya noticed. They had been hinting around to her moving in for over a month.

Sure, I could've asked Amerika to move in, but I didn't. In the beginning, she made it very clear that she didn't 'shack up' with men. She said that she didn't want to live with a man unless it was her father or husband. I respected that shit, but it was time to step shit up. I needed her there every night when I went to bed and every morning when I opened my eyes. I was ready... ready to seal the deal.

For the past few weeks, I had been preparing. I had already gotten Amerika a specially made five-carat diamond engagement ring and booked the yacht with a crew to do the proposal. It was going to be a family affair, so my sister, her husband and her kids were going to come as well. That way, they would be able to keep an eye on Amaya and Javion while Amerika and I tore some shit up in our private suite. I was going to take full advantage seeing that I had paid for the yacht for 48 hours.

The only one that knew what was going on was Javion. He stayed on me about marrying Amerika. Each time he did, I asked about his mother and if he missed his little brother Jaylen. He would answer the same way, "I love mommy and Jaylen, but I'm a teenager and I need you in my life right now... I think you need me too dad."

Javion was right, but that boy was too much. Between him and Amaya, they were too smart for their own self. They kept me busy, especially now that school had just let out. We were preparing for a little outing then.

"Amaya, did you get your swimsuit?" Amerika asked as my daughter busted in the bedroom without knocking. We were definitely gonna have to work on that shit. Until then, I had to remember to lock the door. I wouldn't want my young daughter walking in on me and Amerika in a compromising position that would likely leave her scarred for life.

"Which one?" she frowned, holding two different bright colored one-piece bathing suits.

"Where's the purple one that you begged me to buy you Amaya?" I questioned her raising a brow.

Shrugging her shoulders, she giggled. "I don't know daddy. It was in my room, then it was in the dirty clothes and then it just disappeared!"

That child was so animated, Amerika had enrolled her in drama and dance classes already. That child's schedule was busier than mine.

The past month, I barely had a schedule. Basketball season was over, and I had gotten completely out of the game. I hadn't even told Amerika yet. I wanted that to be another surprise.

"De'vonte! You hear me talking to you?" Amerika asked, snapping her fingers in my face.

"Nah, what'd you say?" I questioned sneaking in a kiss after Amaya dipped out of the room.

"What's on your mind that has you so spaced out?" Amerika interrogated with a skeptical expression.

"I rented this yacht for a couple of days. I wanted to invite my sister and her kids to come to. Kinda like a family gathering."

"Really!" Amerika yelled, grabbing me by my neck. "I get to meet your sister?"

"Shit, she knows everything about you…"

"You talk about me to her?" she giggled playfully hugging me while rocking my body back and forth.

"All the time. Shit, you're my heart baby. You know you stay on my mind. I love you girl…"

"Awwwww, I love you too De'vonte."

That shit melted my insides every time Amerika said that shit. The affect she had on a nigga was crazy!

"When are we going?"

"Next Friday," I said.

"Okay cool," she said as she giggled easing her hand between my legs to fondle my dick through my shorts. "Tell me what I'm thinking right now?"

"The same shit I'm thinking," I whispered feeling my shit rise quickly to attention. "We gotta make it quick though. The kids are waiting."

Locking the door and turning the radio up, I undressed Amerika. My eyes widened as I stared at her naked body. "Damn, you don' lost weight baby."

Although she had slimmed down, her ass and hips had widened. She was sexy and had a glow.

"You are beautiful baby," I acknowledged before making love to her.

That five minutes our bodies connected in ways like never before and left us both satisfied and exhausted. I damn near fell asleep and would have if Amaya wouldn't have come banging on the door.

"Daddy! Daddy, we're ready to go! I found my purple swimsuit!"

"Here we come!" Amerika hollered out nudging me to get up.

Rushing through the shower, we threw our clothes on and went in the den to meet the kids. Javion was in there reading his little sister, 'Where the Wild Things Are'. They were even making scary animal noises.

"I thought y'all was ready?" I teased, dangling my keys.

Javion and Amaya shot by us and beat us to the garage to get in the truck. As I got in, I heard them arguing about Amaya getting in the built-in car seat. She thought she was too damn grown.

"Girl get yo lil butt in there Amaya! We won't be leaving until you're strapped in your seat." I reminded as I hit the control on the sun visor to open the garage door.

"She thinks since she's gonna be four next month, she's too big for the seat dad," Javion tried to explain. Amaya just sat there with her arms folded, not budging.

Amerika intervened by going to the back-passenger door and stared Amaya down. "You know we ain't moving this car until you buckle up right? All princesses wear seatbelts."

"Even queens?" Amaya said softening her frown as she climbed into her proper seat and pulled her belt down, locking it into the chamber.

"Even queens," Amerika smiled and got in the car to buckle up too.

The way Amerika handled the kids without raising her voice was priceless. No matter what they were doing, they always stopped and listened to her.

On the ride to the lake, I stopped by the market to pick up some snacks and drinks. As they all went inside, I stayed in the truck to make a call.

Digging my cell out of side pocket of my navy cargo shorts, I dialed my sister up. She was on vacation for the next two weeks and didn't have shit planned as far as I knew.

"What's up sis?" I chanted as the call connected.

"At home bored with these damn kids. Wish I was somewhere on some water sipping a stiff drink!" she complained.

"Good thing you said that shit because I got some shit planned for this weekend coming up," I began and explained my intentions. She started screaming soon as I told her that I had a ring and I was going to ask Amerika to marry me.

"I'm so happy for you De'vonte!" my sister shrieked. "Amaya talks about Amerika every time she comes over! I can't wait to meet her!"

"You'll love her, especially since she got me to go legit…"

"Nigga! You out the game?!"

"Yes, all the way out, sis!" I assured, listening to her cry.

"I'm so fucking proud of you! I love you, bro!"

"Thanks sis! Love you more!"

Just as I wrapped up my call, Amerika and the kids were coming out. All I could do was smile at the sight of them.

Damn, I love my family…

Chapter Twenty-Six

Amerika

Can life get any better? I wondered as the personal staff greeted us before stepping aboard the huge amazing yacht decorated with silver ribbons and balloons.

"Are we celebrating something dad?" Javion questioned De'vonte with a laugh.

"It's my birthday!" Amaya screamed and jumped up and down.

"Yes, your birthday is coming up! We're gonna celebrate!" De'vonte assured her before scooping her up in his arms.

The gentleman that greeted us, escorted us to our private quarters so that we could change for dinner. De'vonte had us all dress up before having him show us to the formal dining room. His sister, her husband and kids were already there waiting.

Quickly doing the introductions we all sat for a nice meal together as a family. It was nice to mingle with another adult couple with the same goals.

As the kids ate and became restless, some music came on. It was a cover done by Vedo on the song Boo'd Up. I loved his voice and listened closely to his words as De'vonte crept up on me. Clinching onto my hand, he lifted me to my feet and began dancing with me. It was like we were in our own little world.

"You love me?" De'vonte whispered with his cool minty breath blowing in my ear.

"Yes, I love you," I chanted softly, enjoying his hands that were now exploring my body.

"You love me enough to marry me?" he asked pulling back from me and kneeling down before me.

"Look at daddy!" Amaya yelled rushing over to us with everyone else in tow.

"Huh?" I choked up as the tears began streaming down my cheeks.

"Amerika, baby, would you be my queen?" De'vonte asked, revealing a doubled wrap around diamond wedding band with one large stone sitting tall in the middle. It had to be custom made because I hadn't seen anything like it before in my life.

"You wanna marry me?" I gasped, holding out my hand while shaking my head yes. "You're already my king, and yes, yes, yes! I'll marry you babe! Anytime, anywhere!"

Slowly slipping the amazing piece of jewelry onto my appropriate finger, he rose and kissed my lips as everyone cheered even louder. "I love you."

"I love you more and I can't wait to be Mrs. Alexander!" I cried before releasing De'vonte, so I could give everyone else a hug too.

Afterwards, his sister took the kids to their room as De'vonte and I went out on the deck to lay back and look up at the stars. "The sky is so clear and so beautiful," I whispered, cuddling in his arms on the oversized fluffy lounge chair made for two.

"It is and so is my head. This is the best decision I've ever made in my whole life," he explained as he held me and sipped on his drink.

"Oh, yeah?"

"Yeah, and I even have a date set for our wedding. Paid for the reception and honeymoon too…"

"Oh, you just knew I was gonna say yes huh?" I teased and pressed him. "What if I'd said no?"

"I know you love me and my kids. I've been around you long enough to know your heart, your mind and your body. We're in tune and can't nobody fuck that up for us. We've grown to not be only a couple, but a team as well. I love you for that shit ma." De'vonte spoke becoming emotional.

"I do, and this is all I've been thinking about lately," I confessed, thinking about taking our bottle of Crown back to our suite on the other side of the yacht. When I mentioned it, De'vonte was already pulling me up. Yeah, he was just as ready as I was. His dick print gave all that shit away.

"Somebody's ready," I giggled.

"Somebody stays ready," he clowned, taking my hand to fondle him. Groaning out in pleasure, De'vonte began removing my clothes as we busted through our door.

Taking his foot, he slammed it shut behind us. The loud bang forced me into his arms once again. This time knocking him straight to the floor with me on top. I knew my big ass had to knock the wind out of him.

"I'm sorry!" I huffed in a panic as I rolled off. De'vonte snatched me right back on top, ripping my dress in the process.

Whipping his dick out, he slid my panties to the side before straddling me down onto his stiffness. A loud moan escaped my lips as he entered me aggressively. After a few thrust, I relaxed and began to match every one of them. Still almost fully clothed, we engaged in a sensual round of sex, keeping eye contact the entire time. It was like we were consummating the engagement. It was so different than any other time. It had me so caught up, a bitch was about to cry.

I didn't though! Instead, I nestled in my man's chest and passed out in our sticky mess.

*****

The next morning, we both rushed through the shower to meet up with the rest of the family in the dining room for breakfast. As soon as we got to the table, I felt the boat rocking. Now that was a big ass vessel! It had to be well over two, three-hundred feet in length.

Holding onto De'vonte's arm, I became queasy. Feeling a warm liquid about to rise up to my throat, I let go and dashed to the hallway and vomited up every bite I ate the night before.

"Are you okay baby?" De'vonte questioned as he joined me and saw the mess I made.

Lifting up the phone on the wall, he dialed for someone to come and clean it up. "It's probably sea sickness. You wanna go lie down?" he asked.

"Yeah, but I'm hungry. Can you get me some food after you eat?"

"I ain't gonna eat first. I'm gonna walk you to the room and get you settled then go get us both a plate and bring it back. You cool with that?"

"I don't wanna take you away from everyone else babe," I replied honestly. I didn't want to be the damn party pooper. Amaya was ready to go explore on the upper deck and break her piñata that her father had gotten her.

"I'm here for you Amerika. That's what all this is about. It's not about Amaya's birthday. We're going to Disneyland for that. I brought everybody out because I wanted to ask you to be my wife in front of everyone close to me. You are now officially part of my circle."

"I'm honored!" I teased playfully before I became sick to my stomach again.

As I ran to the bathroom, De'vonte yelled out that he was going to get food, bottled water and a ginger ale for my upset stomach. I didn't care what he was getting just as long as it would help with my sudden nausea spell.

Running through the shower after vomiting and pissing myself, I got dressed, washed my soiled clothes out and set the thermostat to 70. I was burning up and hoped I wasn't coming down with something.

Climbing onto the bed, I balled myself up, cuddling with the down pillow. Within five minutes, De'vonte was joining me. "How are you feeling baby?"

"I'm better, but I'm starving. What did you bring?"

While he set all the food down, he stared at me. It was a strange gaze that made me nervous.

"What?"

"Nothing… well, I was just telling my sister how you were feeling and well, ah…"

"What?" I asked, sitting all the way up in the bed. I had to hear this shit. If she was talking about my weight or me eating too much, I was about to flip. "What'd she say about me?"

"She just asked me if you were pregnant…"

My bottom lip dropped. That was the last thing that I thought was about to pop out of De'vonte's mouth.

"No, I'm not pregnant. I just don't feel good, dang," I whined reaching over to fuck up some food.

"When was the last time you were on your period?"

"Honestly, I haven't had a period since getting the shot. I was supposed to go back, but I haven't. Shit, when my period never came back, after my next shot was due, I forgot all about it. I was just enjoying being blood free of the pesky period shit."

"So, you could be pregnant?"

"I highly doubt it De'vonte!" I laughed, still stuffing my mouth.

Not pressing the issue, he came to me and began feeding and coddling me. I immediately knew what he was thinking.

"I'm not pregnant De'vonte!" I insisted, now unsure my damn self. I didn't let on how I was feeling. Instead, I pushed the food to the side and put it on him.

Some good head and bomb ass pussy will have a nigga forget all about why he was bugging you...

Chapter Twenty-Seven

Alondra

I could've shit bricks when Javion called me and told me that he was on some fancy yacht. He sent me pics and all. The one that got me was the one with his father on bended knee in front of Amerika.

"What the hell?" I gasped loudly while zooming in on the photo. "Yo daddy asked Amerika to marry him?!"

"Yes, and she said yes! Mom, she's gonna be my stepmother!" Javion sang happily. I never heard him so excited in my life. It broke my heart.

I wanted to scream, '*what about me*', but I didn't. I just sat on the phone holding Jaylen in my arms crying my eyes out while Javion went on and on about some big wedding that him and his little sister were going to be part of. He didn't even mention his little brother.

"Okay, well you guys have fun. Call me when you get back Javion. I love you."

"I love you too mom. I'll come see you and Jaylen soon," he promised, bringing a smile to my face.

He does love his mama!

As I got out of my feelings, I listened to the doorbell. I knew exactly who it was, but I had no clue he was coming with a surprise…

"Jerron!" I exclaimed when I opened the door. He had bought a beautiful bouquet of flowers and dinner from Olive Garden. I had told him that I enjoyed their pasta.

How thoughtful of him to bring me food. "Thank you so much!"

He walked in with the stuff and I shut the door. "You're welcome. I just thought it would be a nice surprise to bring you some of your favorite pasta. And you're a beautiful woman who deserves to be pampered."

Hearing him say that, I realized how right and true that was. I had been carrying a torch for De'vonte for the longest time. I didn't even entertain the thought of ever being with another man after him. I got involved with Jordan while trying to replace De'vonte. That didn't work out.

Maybe Jerron was the right one to help me forget about De'vonte once and for all. Since I wasn't looking to replace him anymore, Jerron and I might actually have a shot. Over the past couple of months, he had been there for me in more ways than I expected. He seemed to care about me so much, which shocked me because we haven't been knowing each other that long. De'vonte didn't give two shits about me. He had made that very clear with his proposal to Amerika.

I watched as Jerron set the plates of food on the table and poured us some Dr. Pepper. As much as I loved drinking wine with food from Olive Garden that wasn't an option. I was breastfeeding Jaylen, so the last thing I needed was my baby getting drunk because I was careless with my titty.

I sat down at the table and he came around by my side. "Let me go put Jaylen in his crib," he said as he took the baby from me. He kissed my baby boy on the forehead as he made his way down the hall to the nursery. I smiled at that vision because my son would have a father figure in his life. It wouldn't be his biological dad, but at least he'd have a dad.

That meant everything to me. Jerron sat down next to me. "What are you smiling about?" he asked.

"I'm smiling because of you."

"What'd I do?"

"You don't know how much your presence has meant to me these past couple of months. If it weren't for you, I'd be alone. Thank you for being there for me. Thank you," I said.

"You don't need to thank me. I've enjoyed every minute that I've spent with you and Jaylen. I hope to meet Javion one day too."

"Oh really?"

"Yes really. In case you haven't noticed, I really like you Alondra. I know you've been taking things slow because you've been hurt in your past, but I'm here to let you know that I don't want to hurt you. I want you to be yourself with me. I want you to let your guard down and let me in. All I wanna do is have a fair shot at being the man in your life," he said as he stared into my eyes. The shit he was saying had my clit throbbing like my heartbeat was down there.

"That all sounds good, but…"

He tilted my chin with his forefinger and said, "No buts. Just give me a chance." He pressed his lips to mine for the first time and when I say fireworks went off, they went off. By the time we separated, I was ready to jump his bones and get some of that dick, but I refrained from acting all fast ass.

"Um," I said as I cleared my throat. "Well, you definitely have my attention."

"Good."

We ate our food while getting to know each other. It wasn't the same as before. This was a different kind of getting to know you. I was finally ready to let a real one hit it and have it. I just hoped he didn't let me down. "Lord please don't let me down."

My future was finally looking brighter…

Epilogue

De'vonte

Six months later...

Now that I was out of the game, you would think a nigga was bored, but hell no! My life was the total opposite. I had started the wedding plans for Amerika and I but finding out that she was expecting kind of threw a monkey wrench in that. But instead of postponing the wedding like I started to do, I bumped that shit up. She wanted us to be married before she gave birth and that was alright with me. I was anxious to make an honest woman out of her anyway. She and I had been Mr. and Mrs. for almost two months now, and the honeymoon was still going on.

Amaya and Javion were excited to be welcoming a new member into the family and I had to admit that I was just as excited. Amaya had flourished at now four years old. She loved Amerika and her brother, Javion. She was super excited about being a big sister. Javion had grown up so much over the past few months. My son was now a young man and smart as ever. Fatherhood meant the world to me and being a husband was the most awesome shit.

I never imagined that me and Amerika would've taken our relationship this far, but stranger things have happened… like Alondra finding a man and finally leaving me alone. Talk about being the happiest muthafucka alive.

Amerika and I had another four weeks before our twins would make their entrance into the world. Yea, y'all heard right. We were expecting twins, a boy and girl. I had gotten out of the game and was now a family and business man. Life was great!

Amerika

Never in a million years did I think that I'd be this happy. I had the man of my dreams, who was now my husband, and we were expecting twins! Twins! I still couldn't believe it. To say that Amaya and Javion had accepted me as their stepmom with open arms would be putting it mildly. They absolutely loved me, and I loved them.

De'vonte and I had finally gotten Amaya in a good place being without her mom. We took her to the cemetery once a month to leave flowers for Cheryl. I think that was what helped Amaya the most. Every time we took her, she always spoke to her mommy about what was going on with her. I always told her that her mommy was her guardian angel and to remember to close her eyes and Cheryl would be there.

Alondra and I were finally in a great place. She had a new man in her life and we were all thankful for that. She was even invited to my wedding and she showed up with Jerron. They said everything happened for a reason and that day Alondra went in labor was God's way of letting us know that we needed to grow up and put the kids first.

I had to step in and counsel Melinda after her mom died. The young girl was so devastated that I was concerned she might hurt herself. When I noticed her grades dropping, I quickly stepped up. As it turned out, she had been acting up and her grandmother was grateful that I jumped in. Melinda was now in a better place and she knew that her mom was too.

The plans for the school was coming along and I couldn't be more excited. De'vonte had really stepped it up and surprised me. I didn't know that day he walked into my office to discuss his son, I'd end up with him as my husband. I couldn't thank God enough for all my blessings.

Alondra

The Lord was my shepherd and he definitely knew what I needed. He sent me this wonderful man in Jerron and to say that I was happy would be putting it mildly. I was in fuckin' bliss with this man. He had stepped up as my man, confidant, best friend, and father to my baby boy. He and Javion also hit it off and that was something I prayed about. I wasn't sure if they would like each other, but Javion was to happy I had a man in my life. He said he was tired seeing me pine over his father and was glad I had moved on.

I didn't know that shit was affecting my child. I didn't want any negativity around my kids and I was the biggest jolt of negative; at least before Jerron came into my life. Now, I was as mellow as ever. It was amazing what a wonderful man and good dick could do for a female. Lawd! It had turned my life around.

I haven't taken my son to visit Jordan and I didn't plan to. He was in prison for God's sake! There was no way I was ever taking my baby to any prison to see any man. Fuck all that!

Amerika and I were in such a good place. We weren't besties or anything like that, but we were good friends. De'vonte and I were in the best place we had ever been in our entire relationship. I never knew how much stress he had on my life until I let it go. We were now co-parenting our son and behaving like two civilized adults. He and Jerron got along like brothers, which surprised the shit out of me. I didn't expect them to get along, but I was glad that they did.

The four of us were major influences in our kid's lives, so it was super important for us to all be able to get along. God is good.

Jordan

While everyone was on the outside living la vida loca, a nigga was still locked up for a crime I didn't commit. Even though I kept telling those idiots that De'vonte set me up, they didn't believe me. They couldn't find any motive for him to want Sadie dead and frankly, neither could I. They weren't fucking as far as I knew so what reason would he want her dead?

Alondra wouldn't accept my fucking calls and my letters were returned unopened. All I wanted from her was to see my son. She didn't even have to bring him up here; a picture or two once or twice a month would be fine. I heard she had a new nigga and I bet he was playing daddy to my son. I hated that shit but there wasn't shit I could do behind bars.

I had taken the plea deal because I couldn't afford to take the shit to trial. The judge gave me 15 years with time served and I could be paroled in 10 with good behavior. Fuck it! I didn't see a way outta that shit to save my damn life.

God had dealt me a bad hand, but I deserved it. I had fucked over a lot of people, so whatever happened was what happened. I found out a couple of months ago that I had the HIV virus, another reason I tried to reach Alondra. I wasn't sick or nothing yet, but I wanted her to get tested. Hopefully, she didn't have it just in case I kicked the bucket, our son needed at least one biological parent in his life.

Since she didn't want shit to do with me, let her find out on her own. I hoped she didn't have that shit… but if she did, c'est la vie!!

The End!!

Coming Soon...

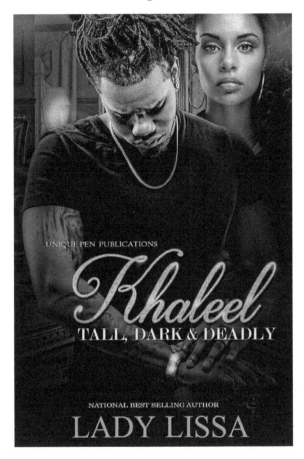

Sneak Peek...

Amerika

Lord knew I didn't need to be involved with that man, but the way he touched me. *Oh God! Why did he have to put his hands on me like that?* The fire that was flaming inside of my lace thong was enough to make my butt cheeks blister. I knew I should have told him to stop, but the words were stuck in my throat. The kisses that De'vonte was putting on me was enough to set my entire soul on fire.

Tell him to stop, this little voice in my head said.

I watched as his kisses trailed down to my stomach. I used to be a little apprehensive about letting a man see me in the nude. I mean, I wasn't one of those skinny or real thin chicks; I was what some called, "on the thick side." Not heavy set thick, but thicker than a king-sized Snickers bar thick. My stomach was somewhat flat, but only because I worked out on the regular. My thighs were real thick and I had a nice fat ass too. My breasts were double D cup sized and, in my eyes, I was the total package.

So what if I wasn't slim…I was still as sexy as I wanted to be. And from the way De'vonte was kissing on me, I'd say that my body was on point to him also.

When he moved his hands along my hips to remove my panties, I grabbed them. He looked at me with hunger in his eyes and asked, "You want me to stop?"

"No, but I think we should," I said, but even I didn't believe the shit that was coming out of my mouth.

While I foolishly debated silently, De'vonte moved his body upward, allowing his swollen member to graze against my thigh. I shuddered at the feel of his dick in his pants. He was still in his clothes. I was the only one who lay there practically in the nude, in just my bra and panties.

"Mmmmm," I hummed as he brushed his lips against mine. The cool spearmint flavor in his mouth made me want even more.

To intensify the oral sensation, De'vonte rubbed his hands along my clit, causing my button to throb beneath his touch. I lightly moaned as he pushed his sweet tongue into my mouth. I readily accepted it as I gripped the back of his head. *Mmmmm, his kiss tasted so good.*

My purring became even louder as I grinded against his left hand that was now inside my panties. Using one finger, he inserted in my honeypot sending jolts of excitement that shot through my body. About to have me lose my mind.

Sure, I had sex before, so I knew what it felt like to be with a man. But, having De'vonte was unlike anything I had ever experienced. He was so thuggish, and his swag was like no other man I had ever been with. He normally wasn't the type of man I would attempt to speak to, with his sagging pants and tatted up body... But, with him, it was definitely different. *Hell, he was definitely different than any other man I had ever dated.* I think that was what attracted me to him.

"You want me to stop?" he asked bringing me back to reality as he continued to thrust his fingers into my moistened center.

I wanted to tell him yes, but my body dared me to. I couldn't even speak as my lips trembled. I was wanting more of that thug lovin'.

Instead of answering him with the words that I couldn't force out if I wanted to, I simply shook my head no. De'vonte wasn't bothered by it. He just smiled as he brought his sexy lips to mine. The kiss we shared that time wasn't just hot, it was searing. That kiss warmed me to my soul.

I enjoyed it until he released my tongue and took his kisses down my body once again. This time when he reached my goodies, he didn't even attempt to remove my panties. He simply pushed them to the side and dipped his tongue between my soaking wet creases. *Oh my God!* I grabbed the sheets as he slowly drove his tongue in and out of my essence.

I wrapped my legs around his neck and prayed that I wouldn't smother him between my thick thighs. De'vonte quickly clinched onto them and I began to grind into his mouth as he devoured me like a homeless man with a bologna sandwich. Within seconds, I could feel myself reaching my peak. He put a halt to it by finally removing my panties.

I watched him as I remembered telling him no. It was too late for all that. Honestly, by then I couldn't even attempt to stop him.

"Let me taste that pussy again without the barrier," De'vonte whispered as he removed my panties and returned to his previous position between my thighs and spread my legs wide. He dove his tongue in so deep, I swear he touched my G-spot. My body shuddered and shivered beneath his tongue as he did some crazy tricks with it.

When I couldn't take it anymore, I released his head from inside my crotch. He brought his lips right up to mine and kissed me, allowing me to taste how sweet my kitty was. Without hesitation, I licked his lips clean as he took my breath away.

Suddenly, De'vonte stood up from the bed and removed his shirt, revealing his toned biceps and six pack abs. He had several tattoos on his arms, chest and a huge one that covered his back. He even had a tattoo on his neck of a pair of red lips. I found that very sensual and sexy as hell. I wanted to press my lips against it, but I was distracted by his next move.

My eyes widened, and my lips released a slight gasp as I watched him unbutton then unzip his pants. He tossed them to the side and climbed back in the bed with me. Scooting near enough for his warm skin to touch me, he stroked my voluptuous body before taking my hand and placing it on his boxers.

Feeling the lump beneath his boxers caused me to become just a little nervous. It had been quite some time since I had been with a man and never with a bad boy. Especially one like De'vonte. He was definitely all the thug I wanted, but I didn't think he was the man I needed at that moment.

As I lay beside him, I wondered if I was at the point of no return or if there was still time to stop before it went too far. I wanted to feel him inside me. Hell, I was anxious to feel him inside me. I wanted to have him touch me down there again. Thug or no thug, I wanted him…

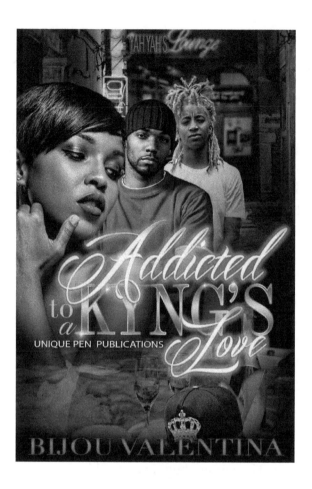

Sneak Peek...

The rain tapped against my window with speed, as the sun was just about completely gone down on the horizon; it made the sky look gloomy with a brownish tint that colored it. I was sitting on my bay window in my studio apartment watching the cars pass by with their windshield wipers swapping on the highest speed, going to where, I don't know? I had my headphones on as I listened to some melancholy jazz as John Coltrane and Duke Ellington's old hit, A Sentimental Mood, played in my ear.

I felt that my life was just like the gloomy dusk scene and the sad jazz song that was playing, all wrapped up in one. I have developed such an old and a dispirited soul.

I've been single for a whole year now, since I broke it off with my now, ex-lover of two and a half years, that goes by the name of Sean. Life with Sean in the beginning, was like magic, the way he swooped me up in his love. He was funny, outgoing, and played the hell out of a bass guitar.

I met Sean one night at a jazz festival that was in town. A few known celebrities were there that I really wanted to see, mainly Jill Scott. I loved the ground that lady walked on, for her music always spoke to my heart and soul.

We were both walking through the crowd that night, heading in opposite directions. Not paying any attention to what was in front of us, we bumped into each other, with him making me spill my drink I had just bought from one of the mobile food trucks that set out amongst the crowd. Standing at 5'11" with an average but bulky body frame, Sean apologized and walked me back to the stand where I got my drink from and bought me another one. Sean's big dark and dreamy eyes, long arrowed nose, dark chocolate skin, and his warm smile was what instantly attracted me to him. We wound up talking all that night long at the festival and enjoyed the show together. We talked so much as we got to know each other a little better, that after the show was over, we were the only two left there at the end of the night.

As time went on, we grew on each other. We spent so much time together until, it just felt like we were meant to be; I thought we'd never part. That was, until I one night we were out having dinner at this restaurant where we sat outside to eat, when a short and stout beautiful woman with caramel skin and hazel brown eyes walked up and confessed to be Sean's wife. She had a nice rock on her finger that blinged like the stars in the sky. The more they went back and forth arguing, the more I realized her stoutness came from her being six months pregnant with their third child. I caught that part she confessed with no problem; it stuck out like a sore thumb.

I wanted to cry and tell Sean how bad he hurt me, and how I couldn't believe he lied to me all that time on how he made me think that he was single in the beginning. I wanted to gouge his eyes out at how he kept his marriage a secret all that time and had me to believe that we were together. Instead, I just got up from my seat, picked up my glass of Arnold Palmer and dashed it in his face and walked away. After that night, I never talked to Sean again.